There's something about being on a plane that I find relaxing. Obviously being squashed into seats made for children and surrounded by strangers isn't it. There's a moment as you pass through the clouds before you reach the blue skies above. Look through the porthole windows and there is a certain serenity. You are where the Gods should be. You are at the total mercy of a metal tube and an overworked pilot who just wants to get drunk and have extra-marital with a prostitute in an upmarket hotel suite. Your life is no longer your own and it's quite liberating. The most you have to consider is whether to have another beer at 8am and upset your better half or settle for the scalding coffee.

I'm not a person of faith, that's not to say I'm an Atheist. They're bigger arseholes than the Catholics. But when you look through those windows you realise, even if it's just for a split second, that it's bigger than you. If there aren't Gods, then it's a great set of coincidences that got us here in this conduit to Heaven surrounded by likeminded fools all secretly praying that that bump won't be the last. That we'll make it to the other side. The greatest and most worrying part of long haul flying is the seat back screens that show the flying stats. I transfix on these, crossing my fingers that the altitude numbers keep going up and the ground speed doesn't drop. There is a sick fucker out there that came up with that idea.

CHAPTER 1.

I met Charlie in a bar near the construction site I worked on. It was on the corner of Copenhagen Street. The bar, not the site. As long as you sat at the back the owner let you smoke inside despite the ban being enforced all over the country. It was the only reason most of the patrons still drank there. Honestly though, I doubt the Police even knew this place existed. The entrance was a simple door next to some run down shop fronts that had long ago closed for business. The only sign that this was a watering hole was the brass plaque with the licensees name on.

I was sat on my own in the corner nursing a double Woodford Reserve when she came over to my table. I had noticed her in there a few times, but she had always disappeared before I had had the chance to speak to her.

'Mind if I use these?' She said waving a box of matches in my face.

'Of course not.' I said. 'As long as I can buy you a drink.'

'I have a drink already. I'll take a seat though.' She sat down. 'You know, I've noticed you staring at me.' She flicked a curl of blonde hair out of her eyes and lit the cigarette. I didn't answer her.

'I'm Charlie.' She said offering her hand.

'Ruben.' I said, taking it.

'So, what do you do Ruben?' She said. 'For a job. How do you pay for all these doubles?' She picked up my glass and looked at me through the bottom. I hated that.

'I'm the Manager of the site at the end of the road.' I replied

'Fancy.' She stubbed the cigarette out half smoked and took mine from the ashtray.

'Not really, it's pretty mundane to be honest.'

'I like your hair.' She said running her fingers over the side of my head. 'You look like a hippy. Is that the intention?'

'Yeah that's why I grew my hair and beard. Except for one problem, all the good weed has gone, and the great bands are either too old or dead.' I moved my head away from her, so she would have to stretch to reach me again. I had no problem with bodily contact or beautiful women touching me. I just didn't know if this girl was crazy yet.

'Wow, cynical.' She said. She took a long drag from the cigarette and blew the smoke into my face. 'You know, you're wrong?'

'Am I? How's that?'

'There's still good weed out there if you know where to look and you always have greatest hits albums.'

I laughed. 'OK, you're one of those. A silver lining girl. And I hate "Best of" albums. They're just the record companies cashing in.'

'What would a silver lining girl be like then?' She lit another cigarette and drained the last of her wine.

'Let me buy you another and I'll tell you.'

She put her hand on mine for a moment but didn't say anything. After ten uncomfortable seconds, I gently slid my hand away and moved for the bar.

'Get me a wine and the same as you. Bourbon always gets me going.'

I looked back at her, but she had already become distracted by two men arguing as they left the bar. 'Yeah Ok.' I called back to the side of her head. She didn't look round.

I nodded a hello to Del the Jamaican as I made my way to the bar. Del had sat in the same seat every evening for the last 2 years since his wife had died. He would sit on his own and get so drunk that around 9pm every night he would piss himself and be thrown out. I felt for this man. He had served in the British Army with distinction and had married his childhood sweetheart and yet here he was, a wreck and only just retired. I once sat and had a drink with him and he told me that he had met his wife, Elizabeth, on the boat to a new life in Britain. They had been some of the first West Indians to come to these shores on the MV Empire Windrush. They were 5 years old on that boat and had been together every day pretty much till the day she died. He said they were never able to have children but that as long as they had had each other nothing else would matter. They had thrown their lot in together and she had died too early. The only way he could cope with the pain and loneliness was to drink so much he lost control of his bladder. They would probably find him in a pile of his own vomit soon.

'Same again please Ryan, and an extra single.'

'Ruben, I'd be careful with that one. She's fucking crazy and she's been through most of the men I know.'

Ryan was a prick. He hated the fact that he worked in the bar. He was an aspiring actor and model. He had a problem though. He was fucking ugly and couldn't act. He had been in a couple of adverts as a teenager so decided to move to London to hit the big time. He didn't and now poured drinks in a shitty pub in North London.

'How's the acting coming along? Any new stuff I should keep my eye out for?'

'Fuck you Ruben. You're jealous that I'm doing something with my life and you're just pissing it up the wall.'

'Put these on my tab please barman.' I turned away and looked over at Charlie, she was singing to herself and drinking the last of my Bourbon. 'Keep living the dream Ryan. It'll happen one day.' I said.

'Cunt.' He replied.

I put the drinks down on the table, Charlie looked at me smiling. She stubbed another half smoked cigarette out. I noticed at least another two in the ashtray.

'Is there a reason why you only smoke half a cigarette?' I asked sitting down.

They weren't cheap and I was starting to think that I'd have to make a run to the shop to get through the evening.

'If you only smoke the first half you don't take in any of the bad toxins. Marlboro put the nicotine in the top of the cigarette to make you want to keep smoking.' She was out of her fucking mind.

'I'm pretty sure they have bad shit in the whole cigarette. Tip to butt.'

'No, you are wrong. A friend told me all about it. She used to work in the factory where they made them.'

I decided to leave it there and change the subject in case she revealed anymore conspiracy theories she may have. Maybe she was the lost Russian Princess.

'So, a silver lining girl.' I started taking a quick sip of my double Woodford. 'Is simply someone who cannot see the bad side of anything. Let's put it this way. If a man loses everything, his money, his home, even his family. You don't see it as the end of his world, you see a chance to rebuild. Start from the beginning, you would say "How many of us get the chance to start again".'

'And what's the matter with thinking like that? Is there not enough sadness already?' She looked pissed so I tried to appease her.

'Nothing.' I said calmly and slowly moving an empty glass out of reach. 'I'm just a bit of a pessimist. I see the real side of the situation. That man's life is fucked. He's going to go through depression. Possibly drug or alcohol addiction. He will lose sight of what it is to be normal and then he'll take an overdose to finally rid himself of the pain.'

She held my hands and stroked my hair again. She looked straight into my eyes. 'You've been messed up by someone haven't you.'

'No, I'm just realistic.' I said moving my hands away from hers.

'No Ruben, you need to stop looking into the awful parts of life. It's a very sad way to be all the time.' She said this in a concerned Mothering tone. 'You must be exhausted. Meet me in the disabled toilet and we'll see if we can make you a little more optimistic about life.'

She finished the wine and took a nip of the Bourbon, stood and straightened her thigh hugging skirt. It was the first time I had had a real chance to see her figure. Fuck I was impressed. The skirt did every justice any women could want from a simple piece of fabric and her shirt was tight in all the right places without looking ridiculous. As she made her way to the back of the bar, I couldn't take my eyes off her arse. It seemed to float. I noticed Del had also sat up to watch the show. Poor old fucker would probably have a stroke with one flick of her eyelashes. She knew how to move. How to make the room stop and stare. I liked it. She disappeared from view. I took a quick scan of the room. Nobody was looking in my direction, so I made my move. Del had gone back to staring into his drink, blissfully unaware of anything happening around him.

I gave a double and a single knock on the door. Not sure why but it seemed the thing to do. Charlie opened the door and pulled me in. It wasn't the biggest of toilets, but it was clean.

There was no piss on the floor, and you could still smell the lemon fresh toilet wipes Ryan had used. How the great fall I thought.

She grabbed my shirt collars and kissed me hard. I felt her hands slip down the front of my shirt. I started to hitch up her skirt when she pulled back and slapped me.

'What the fuck?' I said.

'Do you think I'm some sort of tramp?' She smoothed her skirt out.

'Why else did you get me in to this shitty little toilet?' I was confused and slightly drunk.

'To do a couple of lines of cocaine. I'm not going to fuck you in this rancid dump.' She was smiling which was a good sign that I hadn't already screwed this up.

'You could have said something at the table instead of prick teasing me.'

'I'm not going to fuck you in here but later I will make you scream.' She turned back to the small pile of powder she had poured onto the back of a man's wallet before I had come in and tried to rape her and carved out two neat lines while I rolled a note up. I didn't ask why she has a man's wallet and to be honest I didn't much care. This woman was unbelievable

Later that night at my flat she did make me scream when during a mind-numbing blow job, she inexplicably stuck a finger in my arse. I returned the favour a little while after. She didn't scream in the same way I had.

CHAPTER 2.

I had a place just off the Caledonian Road in North London. It was a bit run down but was cheap due to the fact it was a council flat and the Landlord was sub-letting it to me. It had everything I needed. Running water and electricity when I put money on the meter. I didn't have a TV. Money was coming in and for the first time in years I had savings. I was 26 years old and had managed to avoid any sort of meaningful relationship up until now. That's not to say I had never been in love. I just never had the balls to let them know when I had fallen for them. The notion of having someone around all the time sounded appealing but at the same time terrified me. I thought I had always wanted the whole happy family but had just never got around to it. There was always something better to do. Always someone better to be with. I lived with the constant cliché of drinking too much and always having the black dog following me.

Life with Charlie could be bliss. It was how relationships were supposed to be. There were no weekends with family or dinner dates with friends that neither of us liked anymore but felt an obligation to stay in touch with. We would meet most night's in the bar, eat, drink, then head back to my flat to carry on drinking and fuck. Weekends were spent either in bed drinking and taking some form of narcotics or in a bar doing exactly the same. We were a true dysfunctional couple. Not quite as warped as Sid and Nancy but not too shabby either. For the most part being inebriated was all that mattered. She would go to her work every now and again. But her hours were during the day so every night she would be waiting for me, double whiskey already poured. There were bad times. Of course, there had to be.

My own work had become a harder task of late due to my new Senior Manager who was an arsehole. Mr Stuart Spencer-Wright had blown his way to become Senior Contracts Manager in just 3 years and at 27 was the youngest manager to have a seat on the board of Directors. He had found a loophole in a contract which had saved the company a lot of money. Probably bankrupted someone in the process but who cares about a little matter like that.

The jumped up little shit would drive on site in his "classic" BMW at 8am on the second and last Friday of every month wearing some red cravat and matching corduroy trousers. He would demand to see the cost reports and project reviews. Both of which I knew nothing about. I had lied on my CV to get the interview in the first place and had managed to steer the questions away from anything technical. This little fucker knew that and would try and trip me up at every meeting to prove that I was a lost cause when it came to life as well as my ability to finish the job. We would then have an hour of me being told that I needed to up my game and that he didn't become the youngest manager on the board by going out every night and getting drunk. All I wanted to do was throw up in the bin and down a shot of whiskey to straighten myself out.

Rumour had it his wife was an ex high class prostitute and still turned tricks on the side when they needed money for something. I'd also heard that the double-barrelled name was bollocks too. He had added the Wright to make himself sound more upper class. The man was a top to toe shit. He would sell your kidney if he thought it would get him ahead.

One Friday in particular Mr Spencer-Wright breezed in early to find me leaning out of the window vomiting. Charlie and I had had a fight the night before and the evening had descended into a hate filled slanging match punctuated by heavy drinking and drug taking. She had found an old message on my phone from a girl I had been seeing before her and erupted. The fight had eventually come to blows, from her, and after some make up sex which I'm sure halfway through she had put her hands around my neck I thought it safer to leave and sleep in the office. My flat would be trashed when I got back but at least I'd be alive. And I didn't have too much to destroy anyway.

I sat at my desk. 'You're early.' I said wiping sick off my chin.

'Unfortunately for you, yes.' The look of disdain on his face was masked only slightly by the stupid cravat he held over his mouth and nose.

'What do I owe the pleasure this morning?'

'Ruben this has to stop. I have had Emails complaining that the site is being closed early and that some days you barely turn up at all.' I didn't get a chance to defend myself. 'Morgan Brown Construction has a great reputation that has taken many years to build and I for one won't stand by and let you destroy the hard work of so many others.' It didn't have a great reputation, most other company managers laughed when they found out who you worked for. It used sub-standard materials that didn't meet any sort of standard code and to be fair everything looked like a motorway hotel room. A cheap one. The properties were overpriced and if the Safety Gestapo found out what went on while they were being built the company would be closed down.

'Listen, I've had a rough night. I've had a few problems at home, but I am fully committed to the job.'

He looked at me in disgust. He hated everything about me, but I didn't give a fuck what he thought of me personally. I couldn't lose this job. It had only been a year since I had nearly ended up on the streets. I had been hitting the bottle hard and couldn't hold a job down for longer than a few days. I could barely meet rent every month and with no one to borrow money from I had resorted to dealing drugs to make my way. An old friend of mine was a supplier so it was easy enough to get credit to start up. It wasn't the nicest of ways to pay the bills but the free blow jobs from the single mums who couldn't make their payments on time was a bonus if not a little soul destroying.

'Take a look at yourself Ruben. When was the last time you didn't start the day being sick or needing a drink to be able to get yourself going?' I couldn't remember.

'I'm going to issue you a written warning this time. Complete this project in a suitable fashion and we'll forget about the last few weeks.' He leaned back in the chair knowing it would need an act of God for me to finish on time. I wanted to strangle him with that poncy cravat and bury him in the walls of the building. He spent the next hour telling me that he was a distant relation of Queen Victoria and I spent it trying not to throw up or kill him.

CHAPTER 3.

'Let's get out of the city?' I said.

I was sitting on my chair staring at the ceiling. She was laying on the floor dressed only in a t-shirt, a pair of my boxer shorts and an old pair of socks. She looked hot. She was smoking a huge joint. Charlie liked to smoke the strong stuff that if you weren't careful you could lose days with. I preferred the old fashioned normal weed that you could smoke and still function on.

She passed it to me. 'Because I think it would do us good to get away. We could go out to Kent and rent a room in a little village pub. Wouldn't you like to get out of this bloody place?'

'I can't.' She said. 'I have to work.'

'So, call in sick. Shit I do it all the time when you ask me to. If I didn't call in sick so much, I would lose my mind in that place.'

She looked uncomfortable. 'You don't understand. My boss isn't someone you call in sick to. Especially if you want to keep your job. He'd get rid of you without a second thought and that isn't a very appealing thought at the minute.'

'I'll call him if you want. I'll say you've got dysentery.'

'As lovely as that sounds I don't think so. Pass that back.' I tossed her the joint.

She rolled over and stood up. She looked at me for a few seconds. I thought she was going to say something meaningful. She didn't and walked into the kitchen and took two glasses from the side and grabbed the bottle of Jameson.

'What did you want to be when you grew up?' She said pouring two large measures.

I took one of the glasses. 'Thanks, but it's not even midday.' I put the glass on the floor.

'So? You been acting like a complete pussy the last few days. If you don't want me to hang around just say so and I'll leave. I have other places I can be.'

She took a long hit of the Whiskey. She kept her eyes on me the whole time as if she was waiting for me to give something away in a facial movement. I didn't move. I didn't want her to leave. I liked her. She was a lot of fun and she had made it plain she wasn't interested in doing the whole meet the parents shit. I still didn't actually know what she did for a living. It wasn't any of my business so long as she wasn't stealing from me or asking for loans.

'So where are we on running to the countryside?' I bent down and picked up my cigarettes, took one out and lit it.

'We're not anywhere. I'm not going and I'm not ringing my boss. Just leave it Ruben.'

'Fuck it then, I'm gonna call a few friends and meet them tonight.' I had no friends and she knew it.

'Ok fine, I couldn't give a toss what you do. We're not married. Do what you want.'

She sat on the floor and leant against the wall opposite me. She reached around and picked up some nail polish and started to paint her little finger.

'A Solicitor.' I said.

'What?'

'That's what I wanted to be growing up. I started taking a law A-level and everything. It just didn't work out.' She started laughing. 'What's funny.' I said.

'The thought of you being a lawyer. I couldn't imagine you standing up in court giving a speech. You hate confrontation as well.' She was still laughing.

'Fuck you.' I picked up the glass and downed it in one. The liquid warmed the inside of my throat. 'I would have made a good solicitor. Even if I couldn't stand in court.' I was pissed off.

I stubbed the cigarette out and walked into the kitchen. I opened the cupboard doors. There was no reason to, but I had to do something. She was still laughing. I knew it was the weed, but it was till annoying. I filled a mug with water and sipped it and turned resting my back against the sink. I looked at the damp patch above the fridge freezer, I had been planning to paint over that for months but had never got around to it. I'd go out and buy one of those small rollers you use for behind the radiators and a tester pot of paint.

'So, funny girl, tell me what you wanted to be?' I took another cigarette out.

'If I must tell you, I wanted to be a Nurse, but I never finished school so that kind of put that option out.'

She seemed sad. She took another sip from her glass and stared at the floor as if thinking of what her life could have been. Personally, deep down I think I would have hated being a solicitor. I was quite glad I had been thrown out of college. They had caught me stealing from one of the teachers so was given the option of leaving quietly or being thrown out in disgrace. I had taken the disgraced route rather than admitting anything.

I stepped forward and sat down next to her. She put the joint into the ashtray at her feet and laid her head against my stomach. I felt my fat move and it reminded me that I needed to start back at the gym. I wrapped my arms around her head and pulled her closer to my wobbly mid-section. I thought I heard her cry but when I took a looked down, she wasn't.

'Listen, how old are you? There's always time to retrain. You could go back to school. I don't have much money, but I would try to help out.'

She pulled away and stood up. She kissed me on the lips and smiled finishing what was left in the glass.

'See you've become a complete girl lately.' She topped up both glasses.

'Let's get messed up. Fuck calling in, I just won't turn up. My boss doesn't know where you live so it's not like he's gonna knock, is it?'

I clinked her glass and reached into my pocket for my phone.

'I'll order a pizza and get some coke brought round. Why would it matter if your boss did turn up? I'd just tell him you weren't here and to go away.'

She smiled and kissed me again.

CHAPTER 4.

It had been a couple of days since I had seen Charlie. She had had to go to a seminar near Manchester. She'd told me the name of the town, but I'd been busy that day. My boss had asked for my site diary for the last 4 months, so I had my head in a laptop the whole day making up reasons for why certain things had happened and why we were in delay. I had once been told at school that I would make a good novelist because of my ability to make up stories. I had seriously thought about it for a while but realised that it sounded like too much hard work.

I was sat at the back of the bar in my usual Friday afternoon seat when she came bounding in. She was like an excitable puppy when we hadn't seen each other for a couple of days. The seminars were a regular thing and always seemed to be out of London. I had asked her if she was seeing someone else, but she just laughed and told me not to worry, so I didn't. It was a pain in the arse, but her job paid well. She had mentioned clothes once or twice but nothing concrete. She said it bored her. I decided not to go too much into it.

Sitting down she kissed me for far too long considering we were in public.

'Get me a large wine and a double whiskey. That was one boring trip.' She took one of my cigarettes. 'While I was there a friend was telling me about how Hitler didn't die in Germany and was actually rescued by the Yanks. Supposedly they did it out of spite to us.' I laughed. 'What? This friend of yours really knows her shit. She certainly speaks a lot of it. I have to say that is the best one. It definitely trumps the reason the Titanic sank.'

I got up and kissed her on the top of the head and moved to the bar.

'Hey.' She called after me. I turned to face her. 'The Royal family had to sink that boat. If they hadn't the secret heir to the throne would have made it to America and they would have helped her take the throne. We would have had a World War, a full two years before the first one kicked off.' She was deadly serious.

'Please don't ever say that out loud again. You don't know who's listening.' I mockingly looked around the bar. I smiled and turned away.

'You're a prick.' She shouted.

She was crazy I knew that. I knew it the first time I had met her, but she made me laugh and stopped me feeling depressed all the time. I ordered the drinks with the barman. Wine and cheap whiskey for her, double, expensive bourbon for me. He was new. I didn't like him. He came from Cornwall. Not that I have anything against the Cornish, but they do have a high opinion of themselves. I looked around the bar. I couldn't see Del.

'Hey, has Del been in today?' He looked blank. 'Del the old boy, sits over there?'

'Not sure I know who you mean.' He was a fucking idiot.

'Old Jamaican fellow. Sits in the same seat every day?' Still nothing. 'He piss's his trousers almost every night.'

It clicked in his brain. 'Oh, that dirty old fucker. Ryan barred him the other day. He said he was sick of cleaning up after him.'

'What a nasty shit. This is all the old boy had left.'

'I'm glad. He made the place stink.' He shrugged his shoulders and walked away.

'I hope you never have to get old you prick.'

'Take it up with Ryan, I just work here. I couldn't care less who stops coming in as long as I get paid.' He put the drinks in front of me.

‘Put them on the tab.’ I cupped my hands around the glasses.

‘That’s the other thing. Ryan said to start telling you people that the bar tabs are stopping as well.’

‘What do you mean by “you people?” This place has gone to hell since that snivelling shit became the Manager.’

‘Again, couldn’t care. He said to let you all know that you have to settle any bills you have by the end of the week.’

‘Tell him after the way he’s treated Del he’s lucky any of us still drink in this piss hole. I won’t be paying anything.’ I raised a glass to one of the other locals that I had never bother to get to know. He ignored me.

‘Whatever, like I said I couldn’t give a shit who drinks here. Don’t pay and he’ll bar you as well.’

‘I’d like to see him try. I know the owners.’ I said childishly.

‘So, you know that they sold the place to some Foreign family a few weeks ago. They’re closing the place down next month to renovate.’

I turned and walked away without answering. Another good pub gone I thought. I placed the drinks down in front of Charlie. She was whispering into her phone while trying to light a cigarette and failing. I took the cigarette from her lit it and passed it back to her. She smiled then went back to her covert conversation.

‘They’re closing the pub down.’ I said hoping she’d hang up. ‘Gonna turn it into some brasserie probably.’

She ignored me so I lit a cigarette for myself and took a sip of my bourbon. She drank her whiskey in one. It annoyed me that she never enjoyed the whiskey. I had never once seen her take her time over the first drink. That was the best bit of whiskey drinking. The warmth fills your mouth before slowly soothing your throat and giving you the feeling that your stomach is being cuddled. After the first you lose that experience and then it just feels like someone is wrapping a huge towel around your brain.

She slammed the phone down on the table. 'I've got to go to work tonight.' She said

'For fuck sake. I haven't seen you in days. I was looking forward to spending some time with you.'

'Trust me Ruben the last thing I wanted to do was go back to work tonight.' She started muttering under her breath.

'Tell them you can't make it. Tell them you have plans.'

'I just tried. It's not that easy.' She started on her wine.

'Yes, it is. Or just don't turn up again. What's the worst your boss will do?'

'Just leave it Ruben. I'll only be a few hours anyway.' She paused to sip her wine and stub the cigarette out. 'I'm off till Wednesday from tomorrow so I was thinking we could go to the countryside like you wanted. Not Kent though. I don't like Kent'

She was worried about something. She picked the nail polish on her forefinger with her thumb nail when she was in deep thought or depressed. I had mentioned it after noticing her do it once before. She told me to mind my own business. A strange response I thought.

'What's the matter with Kent? I like it there.'

'What about Oxfordshire? I've never been there. You can take me to a fancy restaurant, and we can stay in a country pub with a huge duvet and views of the fields.' She perked up a bit at the thought of the huge duvet.

'Ok, I'll try and book us somewhere later.' I leant across the table and kissed her. 'I'm not sure about the posh restaurant though. I get nervous and stutter.'

We sat and talked for the next hour about how much I hated my job and boss. I liked talking about me and my problems.

Other people's worries bored me. By the time she had finished her final drink I was well and truly shot and had slumped into the seat. She stood and straightened her clothes, my mind raced back to the first time she had done that in here. It seemed like an age ago now. I was falling in love with her. She bent down and kissed me gently on the lips and again on the head. She held her hand on my face for a second longer then turned and walked out.

CHAPTER 5.

Charlie had been quiet since she had gotten back from work a few nights before. She had walked into a cabinet drawer a colleague had left open and now sported a huge black eye and split lip. Her boss had given her an extra week off. Which was a bonus. That night she had slept in the chair rather than come to bed and wake me. When I woke at 7am I found her with a half-drunk bottle of Jameson between her legs and my last few Amitriptyline gone. That had pissed me off. Getting prescription drugs at the moment was difficult as my usual contact had been arrested a few months earlier.

'Fuck sake Ruben. How many times do I have to tell you to top up the electricity card? You're a child. There's no hot water again.'

'Get yourself dressed and I'll nip to the shop and get some. I've booked a Hotel for a couple of nights. You'll like it.' I answered from the kitchen scrabbling for my wallet.

'Where's the Hotel?' She replied coming into the kitchen pulling one of my T-shirts over her head.

'A little village a few miles outside Oxford. Have you heard of Le manoir?'

She got excited.

'How have you managed to get a table there? I thought you didn't like those types of places?' She threw her arms around me.

'Fuck no, I haven't booked a table there. I'm not made of

money. The Hotel is a little pub in a village near there.'

She let go of me. She didn't look as impressed as I had pictured.

'So why mention Le manoir at all then? You could have just stuck with "the Hotel is in a little village near Oxford" I would have been happy with that.' She had a point.

'I'm going to the shop. Want anything?'

'Cigarettes. Please.'

I kissed her on the forehead and left the flat. Thinking of what I would need to take with us I didn't see the racist old lady who lived in the flat below.

'Hello..' I could never remember her name.

'Hello dear. How are you?' She held my arm. 'I haven't seen you for a few days. I thought you had moved out.'

I moved my arm away from her. 'No, just been busy with work and stuff. You know how it is.'

'I knocked on your door the other night, but no one answered. I knocked pretty hard a few times dear.' I wanted to tell her to fuck off and die.

'Oh, was that you? I thought the Jehovah's had got in again.'

She leaned in closer and held my arm again. 'I told them to piss off the last time they came knocking.' She put her over her mouth and leaned in closer still. 'You know most of them are of the dark persuasion?' That was my cue to push her down the stairs.

'Anyway, I'm in a bit of a rush. I'm going away for a few days.' I pulled my arm away again.

'Say no more. I'll keep an eye on things.' She winked at me and stroked the side of her nose like we had a secret thing going on.

I made my way down the stairs and away from the old Nazi. I wondered who's side she had been on during the war, probably a collaborator. The first time I had introduced myself she had asked if I was Jewish because of my name. I should have told her to fuck off then.

I stepped into the shop. I asked for two bottles of Jameson's, cigarettes and topped up the electricity card.

I crept back up the stairs to the flat, I couldn't face another meeting with the old lady.

'What took you so long?' Charlie said as soon as I opened the door.

I didn't answer.

'Well?'

'I bumped into Himmler's little sister on the stairs. She really isn't a very nice person you know. You know I'm certain she was the one who shopped Anne Frank.'

She smiled. 'I don't know why you speak to her. She asked me if I'd seen the "dirty looking little fucker hanging round" the other day.'

'Who was she talking about?' I said putting the electricity card in the machine. The lights came on.

'The little Romanian woman who cleans the communal areas. She said not to trust her, or she would steal my gold teeth.'

'You do go flashing those things around.' I said.

She laughed. She had stopped doing that too often lately. I made us a cup of coffee each and watched her as she packed the bag for us to take. I lit a cigarette and rolled a couple of joints for the road.

'Have you bought any coke for this weekend?' She asked

'I forgot. I have a couple of grams in the bedroom we could take.' I sipped the coffee. 'To be honest I thought we could have a weekend without it.'

'Why? You really have turned into an old woman lately.'

'Do you not think we have been hitting it a bit hard in the last few weeks? I mean I can't remember the last Wednesday night I was in bed before 1am.'

She looked at me like I was ill.

'Well fuck you, I'm taking it. I'll bring you some of my pants to wear. Maybe a little black number.'

'Don't be sarcastic. I'll make a call.'

I called my dealer. I only ordered a few extra grams. He said he would be an hour. We sat for a few hours talking about the weather and what food we would order when we got there. It was nice and normal.

'Listen, its 2pm already. Why don't we give the trip a miss and stay in for the weekend?' She said

'How about no. I've booked the room, I'm going. If you hadn't wanted Cocaine we would nearly be there by now.'

'It's not my fault you have a shit dealer who is always late.' She screamed at me.

'Don't you blame Nickoli for this. He's one of my best friends.'

'He is a drug dealer who you sit and get stoned with. He is not your friend. You don't have any friends you whimpering wanker.'

My phone rang. It was Nickoli. He was downstairs. I went out and met him and took the drugs back to the flat.

'Let's just get in the car and go.' I said.

'I don't want to go now. You've ruined it. Give me the powder.' She replied. Her eyes were blank.

I threw the drugs to her and she immediately poured one of the wraps out on the table and began cutting it into lines. I instantly felt sorry for her and wanted to blow the drugs onto the floor.

'I still want to go.' I said as she handed me a rolled note. I took it and inhaled the line.

'See it'll be a lot more fun staying here. We haven't got to go all the way to Oxford to relax.'

'I need a break Charlie. What with work and not sleeping, I need to have a time out. I thought you wanted to get out of London?'

'Why would you think that?'

'Because you said you wanted to get out of London not a few days ago.'

'Are you seeing someone else?' She inhaled a line. 'Is that why you're lying?'

'What the fuck are you talking about? You're crazy.'

'You are. You piece of shit. That's why you want to get me out of London. I bet she's on her way, here isn't she?'

She jumped to her feet and raced to the window looking up and down the street outside. Convinced no one was there she marched back to the table and sat down without speaking. I put my hand on hers and kissed her on the forehead. I didn't say anything, I just picked up my bag turned and walked out. As I closed the door, I heard the glass smash against the kitchen wall and her inhale another line. I stepped on to the pavement, reached inside my coat and pulled out one of the joints I had rolled before. Lighting it I pulled deeply letting the smoke fill as much of my insides as possible. I looked up and down the street, not for any reason, it was something that I always did, and Charlie had done it, so I was paranoid now. I walked the two roads up to where the car was parked and threw the joint stub into the drain, it had started to rain. I opened the door and got in. I'd go to Oxford and try to relax on my own. Hopefully I'd be able to sleep for more than a couple of hours. I looked into the mirror, my eyes were drained, my hair and beard was in serious need of cutting.

CHAPTER 6.

I knew I was dreaming. Charlie was there, her hair thrown on top with just a few straggling blonde curls hanging down. She was cuddling a baby and crying. I couldn't see the baby's face. I looked around the room, it was my lounge. My old armchair, an empty bottle of whiskey on the floor, a packet of Anti-depressants on the arm. Definitely my flat. I tried to touch her shoulder but missed somehow. Looking at my wrists there were deep cuts still seeping. I screamed her name, but she didn't move she just kept crying. I looked around the room again there was a TV on, the news was talking of another terrorist attack, this time they had brought down another plane on a city in the Far East. I looked back at Charlie, she had stopped crying and was facing me. Her beautiful face was bruised and cut.

'Why did you leave us?' She screamed at me. 'Why?' She started ripping at her hair and suddenly rushed at me the baby had disappeared. I woke sweating. It took a moment to realise that I was in the B&B room. I switched the flowery light on and looked round the room, no mad woman or crying baby.

I got out of bed, opened the window and lit a cigarette. I had suffered from nightmares since I was young. I used to lay in bed as a child terrified and unable to move while a man would stare at me from the open doorway. He never said anything or came any further into the room, just stared. It was either him or I would wake to find an elderly man and a little blonde girl standing next to me. The girl would smile, and they would talk to each other in a language I couldn't understand. Then they would walk out of my bedroom without looking back. They came a couple of times a week and even now that I was in my twenties, I was still haunted by them on a regular basis. It was no wonder that I drank myself to sleep now or didn't sleep at all. My Mum told me a story that she once stood at my door and watched me have a full conversation in a pitch perfect American accent with the end of my bed. When she asked who I was talking to I replied that I was talking to Wally my friend.

I flicked the cigarette out the window and crossed the room back to the bed. Sitting down I took a long swig from the bottle of whiskey. My watch read 2.33am. I laid down and tried not to think of the dream. I thought about calling Charlie, she would be up, probably smashing my flat to pieces and burning some clothes. I took another swig and got up and put some jeans on. Sitting at the small side table I picked up the book I'd brought. It was a short story collection by Raymond Carver. It wasn't bad.

The B&B was nice. Friendly staff and good Ale on tap. Something you didn't get too much of in London. I spent the whole day in the pub reading, the only time I put the book down was to go outside for a smoke. I did take one long walk to smoke a joint and found an old monastery. I wasn't sure if they still had monks there, so I sat on the wall and finished the joint to see if any came out. After an hour none did. That was pretty much all the village had so I went back to the pub and holed up in the corner again.

'I'm going to check out early if that's OK?' I said.

'That's a shame Mr Humphrey. I do hope everything was OK with the room.'

'Yes. Fine. I have to get back to London for a work thing.'

'Such a shame, will you be leaving us tonight or the morning?'

'It'll be the morning, I've had too much to drink to leave tonight.'

She rustled some papers and pressed some buttons on her hidden computer.

'You will have to pay the full amount Mr Humphrey.' She said

‘No worries and please it’s Ruben.’

I settled the bill and went back to bar. I ordered some food and a pint of ale and found another seat. The pub had started to fill up with locals. Christ knows where they all lived as I had only seen a dozen houses in the village, but they all knew the bar staff by first name.

On the way back to London I stopped at the shopping village and saw Elizabeth Hurley walking through with her entourage. Very attractive in the flesh. Then I left.

CHAPTER 7.

After getting back from Oxford I had managed to get my act together. Charlie had been gone when I returned and to be fair the flat wasn't in too bad of a mess. She had broken a couple of my old vinyl's, but they were only some ZZ Top that someone had left at the flat a while ago. I had hidden all my original Zepplin and Stones LP's behind my wardrobe. It could have been a whole lot worse. The trip to Oxford and the few days without Charlie there had given me a bit of breathing space to think about what the fuck I was doing with my life. I didn't want to end up in a gutter with a tramp looking for a warm hole to slip into. The drinking and drug taking had to be almost solely reserved for weekends and I had to somehow turn the project at work around and back on schedule. It would be to the delight of my little arse of a boss, but it was the future I needed. The clouds had been gathering over head for some time.

Charlie had become more neurotic in the week or so leading up to and after the trip. Her wild outbursts were more frequent and brought on by the most random of events. She was certain that I was seeing someone else due to my talk of slowing down all things narcotic. In her eyes, it could be the only explanation. The first day she came by after Oxford she had thrown a glass at my head because I had eaten the last of some ice-cream that had been in the freezer. Her drinking had started to be more of a problem too. Every night she was drinking both our share and falling into a drunken coma. I would have to lift her on the toilet before rolling her in to bed. I lost count of the nights I would sit, stroking her hair and watching to make sure she didn't choke on her own vomit. She would mumble incoherently, never quite waking and never completely asleep, there were dark places inside her head. I was a selfish arsehole who had no desire to find out what those demons were. I had my own to contend with. She was exhausted and so was I. In the morning, it would be the same routine. I would argue that she was drinking too much and that I wouldn't sit and watch her kill herself. She would say it was because I was working all the time and that she was lonely and hated her job. To be honest I couldn't take much more of the baggage that came with her.

CHAPTER 8.

I hadn't seen or spoke to Charlie for a few days and was on the verge of calling the Police when she burst through my office door one morning. She was drunk and high on something.

'Where the fuck have you been? Charlie, you can't just disappear for days like this anymore. It's ridiculous.' She sat down and stared at me. Her eyes were vacant.

'I hate you, you made me do it.' There was real venom in the tone of her voice.

'What have you done? What have I done?'

'You fucking know what you did. It's her isn't it? That disgusting whore.' She sprang out of her chair. I flinched back thinking she was going to throw something.

'Charlie sit down. I have no idea what you're talking about.'

'You know. You're no better than any of the rest.' She started pacing the floor. 'All you want is to fuck me and leave me.' Her pacing quickened, and she started muttering to herself. 'He knows. Of course, he knows. I thought I could trust you.'

I signalled for the contractor I'd been having a meeting with before Charlie burst in to escape. The poor bastard was routed to his chair in fear of this crazed women. He virtually ran to the door to get away. Charlie was so far gone she hadn't even realised he was sat right next to her. Her muttering had got unnervingly quiet.

'He knows what he's done. They all know.'

'Charlie who are you talking to? Sit down please.' I had started to panic. 'Tell me what I have supposed to have done. Who have you been speaking to?' She lurched towards the desk her face no more than an inch from mine. I almost screamed in fright.

'You know.' I looked into her eyes there was no one home. This beautiful woman who I thought I was falling in love with had become like a deranged animal. She turned for the door.

'Charlie wait. You can't leave like this. Let me get you a cab to take you home.' She turned back and had tears on her cheeks. 'I had to sleep with him, or he wouldn't give me the stuff. He wanted to know where I had been staying.' She took the few steps back to where I was sat and knelt beside me. 'Do you promise that I'm the only one? That she didn't mean anything?'

'Who?'

'Why did you fuck her Ruben?' I opened my mouth, but nothing came out. I was shell shocked. She left before I could muster a sound. She couldn't have known. I grabbed my phone and searched through the old messages, nothing. I thought of going after her when I looked down at my work phone. I went to the messages and scrolled down through the past couple of weeks. I found it.

"Great time this evening. Will work late every night if that's the bonus I can expect." Fuck I thought.

The message had been from the Admin girl I had slept with a few times. Stuart had organised her to help me with the paperwork side of the project. I had always been so careful and deleted anything to do with her. She only came to site every couple of weeks and was absolutely stunning. She was also Stuart Spencer-Wright's cousin. Which coincidently was the only real reason for me wanting to get her into bed in the first place.

It hadn't taken a lot of effort to get her pants off and for me fucking a member of his family was as good as taking a shit on the bonnet of his prized BMW.

Alysa would arrive in my office every other Thursday to put

together the paperwork ready for meetings and my visit from Stuart. Once the usual bullshit was out the way I would lock the door and get out a bottle of whiskey. I was using her for any information I could gather to have some kind of leverage against him. She was using me as a bit of rough. I was happy with the arrangement.

The week before this she had arrived and gave me the Holy Grail of inside information on Mr Spencer-Wright. We hadn't made it to the whiskey, she had grabbed me as soon as the door was locked. She kissed me hard and bit my lip.

'I want you to fuck me Ruben. I've been thinking of you all week. I want to feel you inside me.' I grabbed the back of her hair and pulled her to me. Kissing her I slipped my hand into her pants. She was already dripping wet.

'Do you want me to suck your dick?'

'Knock yourself out.' I replied.

She sank slowly to her knees the whole time keeping eye contact with me. Not normally something I like. It made me feel nervous and uncomfortable. She undid my trousers and pulled them down. Her tongue ran up and down my now almost bursting penis just stopping long enough at the tip to make the muscles in my arse spasm. After a few strokes, she stood.

'Now fuck me.' She whispered. She turned, lifted her dress and leant over my desk. I moved up behind her and eased her underwear to one side and slowly pushed in as deeply as I could. She let out a small groan as I began to slide in and out. The warmth of her almost made me come straight away. I slowed down.

'Pull my hair back.' She panted.

As I reached across to grab a good handful of hair Stuarts' business card caught my eye. I picked it up and read it 'Senior Contract Manager, Board Member'. The pretentious prick.

'This one's for you, you cunt.' I said under my breath. I picked up the pace and pounded Alysa as hard as I could. Just as I came, I threw his card in the bin.

A minute or two later we were sat on the floor with a large whiskey each and sharing a joint.

'That was good.' I said.

'Thank you.' She replied sipping her drink. 'You got a bit rough for a bit there. It felt like you were putting some hate into it.'

'No, just thought I'd speed things up a bit.'

'Oh right. You know Stuart bent me over his desk like that on my first day. He was a lot like you were at the end there. Very forceful.'

'I beg your pardon.' I thought I'd miss heard.

'He said it was his way of showing me he was in charge.'

'Jesus. I'm sure that qualifies as rape Alysa. I thought I had it bad with one of his arduous speeches.' I couldn't believe my ears, I finally had a stick to beat the jumped up little shit over the head with.

'Oh, don't worry it wasn't the first time.' She replied. I took a drag of the joint, maybe it was the weed making me hear things.

'We have been having...' She paused searching for the right words. If there were any. 'Relations for years. He was the first person I slept with. Now he's my boss so we have had to stop seeing each other.'

'Because he is your boss is not the main reason you need to stop. It's fucking disgusting as well. That's a better reason and I'm sure it's incest.'

'Not between cousins it's not. It always seemed the most natural thing.'

'I don't think your family would see it as natural. I think they would agree with me and confirm it's fucking disgusting.' I was open to most things slightly depraved or otherwise, but I had to stop the bus at screwing your own family. I stood up and stubbed the joint out and looked for my cigarettes. I needed to clear my head.

'I thought I was in love with him for a while. Maybe I am but I know it'll never work out. There are too many people with an opinion.'

'People do like to have an opinion on these things.' I re-lit the joint and tried to think. 'Listen, we can't do this anymore. It was different when I thought you were just his family but if you're sleeping with him. It makes me feel a bit uncomfortable'

'Why do we have to stop? I've just said that I am not seeing him anymore.' She reached up and took the joint from me.

'It's not just him, I have Charlie to think about. She hasn't been herself lately. I think she may be back on hard drugs.'

'So, fucking what. It hasn't bothered you up till now that your girlfriend is crazy. And are you kidding me with the hard drugs shit? You have both been on those since I first met you. It's because you can't handle the fact that I have slept with Stuart.'

'As natural as you think it is, it's not. It's ever so slightly perverted.' She dropped the joint in her glass, stood and straightened her clothes.

'So, you have the juicy gossip to finally get him off your back and now there's no need to keep fucking me. You can go back to being concerned about that mental case you do or don't live with.' She put the glass on the desk and bent down to pick up her bag.

'He's your cousin you sick fucker.' I was angry that she thought she could take a swing at Charlie. She snatched the glass from my hand and for a moment looked like she would hit me with it.

'The drink and drugs doesn't solve your problems Ruben. I'm sure I'm not the first person to tell you that and I guess I won't be the last. You're genuinely a nice person when you're not acting like a child and trying to prove how detached and tough you are. Stop being such an arsehole just once or twice in your life.' She downed the last of my whiskey, handed me back the glass and left. It would be the last time I saw her.

I sat at my desk, lit a cigarette and took a swig from the bottle. I probably shouldn't have called her a sick fucker. She was a nice girl really and it was a shame that we had to of met in this way, but life can be a fucker sometimes. I had something on Stuart now and just had to pick the best moment to use it. Or I could just forget it and protect Alysa. Obviously, that would be the gentlemanly thing to do.

CHAPTER 9.

I sat at the breakfast bar that doubled as the dining table in my kitchen and picked up the phone to call Charlie again. I was beginning to worry about her. It had been nearly 2 days since the incident in my office and I still hadn't been able to get in touch with her. It had dawned on me that even though I had been with her for a good few months I knew nothing about her. There had been a few bits of the back story. She had grown up in the leafy Kent suburbs only a few miles from the part of South East London I had been dragged up in. She had said both her parents were dead and didn't have any brothers or sisters. Both statements I didn't really believe. She had had a few boyfriends but nothing serious. I knew she was a bit mental but anyone who spent more than five minutes in her company could tell that. Other than that, she was a bit of a ghost. I had never met any of her friends. I wasn't even sure she had any. She had only mentioned one person and I couldn't remember their name. She had said she worked in clothes shop somewhere in the Brick Lane area but had never told me where and I had never been too bothered to find out. She talked about the seminars she went to were for fashion and buying the new trends. I had no idea whether she was telling the truth and as long as I didn't have to go, I didn't care.

I sat back on the stool and took a bite of my toast and noticed a burn mark on the worktop. I tried to think of where it came from. She would turn up sooner or later, she always did, but I couldn't help worrying. She was out of her mind that day and I still had no idea who the man was she had mentioned or what she had had to do. She could have been dead in an alley for all I knew. I rubbed at the burn mark. It looked like a frying pan shape. I hoped the landlord wouldn't notice or I could forget getting my deposit back. He was a piece of shit.

I thought about how I would explain the message should she ever come back. It could simply be that she had been mistaken. That I had simply bought Alysa a bottle of wine for all the help she had given me and if she read the message again it would be clear that nothing had happened between us. Charlie would be thrilled and also a little embarrassed at all the fuss she had made. Of course, I wouldn't want to make a big thing of it. We would then have great make up sex and all would be forgotten. I could put on a record and we could spend the afternoon getting stoned in the armchair.

I was a fucking idiot for thinking that would work but I needed some hope. I made some coffee, finished my toast and smoked two cigarettes. I looked at my watch. It was already nearly noon. I called Stuart and told him my Nan had been taken ill and that it didn't look good. He told me to take the day off and that he would take care of things. He had recently lost his own Nan so I knew he would be sympathetic if I used that excuse. I hated Mondays at the best of times. When I was a few years younger I had a job and had managed to get out of working every Monday for four months.

I needed to speak to someone I could trust so, left the flat and avoided the old racist lady. I couldn't face spending the next hour discussing how it wasn't the same round here with all the different colours moving in. Or how we needed another war to sort the men from the boys.

The VW Golf started first time. You had to love German engineering, I hadn't used the car in a couple of weeks and most old cars would have been dead. I often thought where the World would be if the Germans had won the war. Ok we would all be living under the fascist Nazi fuckers, but can you imagine what they would have achieved in engineering? I called my Dad on the way back across the Thames to make sure he was in.

'What's the matter?' He said when he finally answered.

'Why would anything be wrong? I just thought I'd come over and see you.'

'Ruben, you haven't called in a month or visited in over 4 months and you only come South of the water when you have a problem, or you have fucked up again.' The divide between South and North London still amazed me. They were like two separate countries to the people who lived on either side of the Thames. I preferred the North to be fair, not that I would admit that to my Dad.

'Dad I need advice. Where will you be in an hour?'

'You're a fucking clown. Meet me at the shed. I'll tell your Mum you'll be staying for dinner.' He hung up before I could protest.

The shed was on his treasured allotment. Now semi-retired he spent almost every afternoon there. I loved the man beyond question, not the most talkative and I barely saw him growing up due to his insatiable work ethic. He was always there when I needed him though and would do anything to give me what I needed.

He had left school at 15 and gone straight into construction. Money was tight growing up, but I never went without and had more than most of the poor bastards on my estate. He was a hard man, he had been taught by his Dad not to show pain to anyone and the best cure for illness was work. I know I disappointed him in that regard. He had once gone to work with the flu in the middle of winter so he could pay for Christmas. He ended up with Pneumonia and had to be rushed to Hospital. I still remember eating egg and chips for Christmas dinner, my Mum couldn't cook the usual dinner due to him being in a such a state and the rest of my family were arseholes and never offered to have me for dinner. I dipped my chips in the yoke listening to him screaming upstairs for what felt like hours. His temperature was so high he was hallucinating that giant spiders were trying to get him.

I parked up in front of the allotment gates and walked down to my Dad's plot. It was only April and still quite cold. I put my jacket on and a hat for good measure. My Dad stood in the middle of his potatoes in dirty jeans and a T-shirt.

'Cold?' He said. No hello's or hug's.

'Yeah. You should at least put a jumper on Dad. I'll end up having to bury you out here if keep dressing for summer at this time of year.' He ignored me.

'No work today? What excuse did you give this time?' He took a seat on a half broken deck chair and opened a beer from an ice box hidden underneath. He didn't offer me one.

'No, I'm fine. I had a bottle of water on the way.' I said.

'Good because there are only enough for me and Jim over there. You wanted a beer, you should have brought some.'

'So, what did you tell them?' He handed me a bottle and smiled.

'I said Nan had been rushed to hospital.'

'You're a fucking delight.' He said. 'So, what's wrong? I haven't got any money to lend you if that's what you're after.' He waved Jim over for a beer. His allotment friend. Nice old man, bit of a nonce around younger women.

'I've got money. It's Charlie, she's completely lost it this time. I think she's left me, but I can't get in touch with her so I'm not entirely sure.' He cut me off.

'Right, stop talking like a little girl and start by telling us who Charlie is and what you did to make her leave?'

'Why do you think that it would have been something that I had done?' I said insulted.

'I love you Ruben, but you act like a child. Every relationship you have had you fuck up by putting your dick where it has no place being.' He had a point. Jim raised his bottle in acknowledgement.

'What was the Indian girl's name? You remember, you completely screwed her over.' He said. Jim started tapping his leg as if thinking about it.

'Jim why are you trying to remember you never met her. It was Saanvi.' I replied.

'I might have known her name, you little shit.' Jim stuck in before my Dad could carry on.

'Saanvi that's right.' My Dad scratched at his 2 day old stubble.

'She was stunning. Jim, she would have given up her whole family for him.' He said

'Yeah they didn't approve of me being White and working class. Which is your fault I think.'

'If you remember you slept with her cousin and got so drunk at her brothers, wedding that you threatened her Grandad. The man was 80.' He shook his head. 'It was a dry wedding as well.'

'It was definitely the working class thing.' I countered.

'I saw her a couple of weeks back.' He said. 'She's married to a solicitor and finishing her last year to become a Psychologist. Still beautiful.'

'That's good to hear. I really fucked up there. I wish I had been older when I meet her.'

'What like now?' They both laughed.

We sat in silence for a few minutes. I lit a cigarette; my Dad tutted his disapproval. He had never smoked and hated the fact that I loved to. I thought of Saanvi and the life I could have had. I could have been the solicitor she married, not the one needing a solicitor from time to time.

My mind went back to Charlie. She was the reason I had made the trip back to the South. I threw the cigarette into the potatoes patch and began telling him how and when I had met Charlie. I left out the fucking and drug taking parts. He didn't need to hear those details. I poured my heart and mind out for 20 minutes until I go to the part about Alysa.

'You see it was just to get at my boss. He's the one to blame really. If he hadn't been such a wanker I wouldn't have slept with his cousin and Charlie and me would still be happy.' My Dad and Jim were looking at me. They had been engrossed in my story, only losing attention when the beer bottles ran dry and they had to open another. Jim started laughing first then my Dad joined in.

'What are you laughing at? How is any of this remotely funny?' I was furious.

My Dad spoke, tears streaming down his face. 'The only sad part about this whole sorry affair is there is some poor girl out there in pieces, doing God knows what because she thought she could trust my degenerate of a son to keep his dick to himself.'

'That's lovely Dad. Thanks for the support.'

'What kind of response were you looking for? Do you want a hug and to be told everything will be ok?' He put his empty bottle down. 'This is your making Ruben. You were big enough to screw this girl over, you'll have to be man enough to put things right again or deal with the outcome.' He leaned down to grab another bottle but only found the empty box.

'You really want my advice?' He sighed.

'Please Dad, I don't know what to do. How do I make this right?'

'Finding her would be a good start.' Jim thoughtfully said. He pushed himself to his feet patted me on the shoulder and went back to his own little plot laughing at his parting shot. I lit another cigarette and inhaled deeply.

'Ruben, these women you treat the way you do, it's not fair. They are not extras in some shitty film about your life. They have feelings as well. Do you not think they deserve to be happy? These are their lives as well and you should respect that. Your Mother and me, we brought you up better than this, you can't just go around using people and then discard them when you become bored or distracted by something or someone else.' He looked under his seat and found two more bottles. He gave one to me.

'I've tried to be like you. I've tried to be faithful, to be happy with one girl. It just isn't as easy as it was for you and Mum. There's more pressure today. Women want more from you. They want you to be open about how you feel, and I can't do that. You don't understand.'

'Don't be fucking ridiculous.' He snapped back. 'Do you really think we had it any easier? Trust me boy your feckless generation have never had it so good. Where was our gap year? We couldn't jump on a plane to the other side of the world because life had got a bit shit like you can. Your Mum and me worked bloody hard every day to raise you. It killed me to watch your friend's families going on holidays and buying new cars knowing we couldn't afford them.' He took a sip of his beer and took a deep breath. 'But as long as I had you and your Mum not being able to have all the materialistic bullshit didn't matter as much. We loved and respected each other and, in the end, that's all that matters.'

I tried to think of something to say, something that would put me in the right again. 'What about being open and honest? Am I supposed to break down in tears every 5 minutes?'

'Sorry I forgot you're too tough, too closed off and mysterious to talk about how you feel. Grow the fuck up will you. Do you think your Mum has never seen me cry? I told her all my dreams and fears for the future. Despite only most of my fears happening and not too many of my dreams she still loved me.' He took a sip of beer. 'Life is short Ruben and the way you are going it's gonna be a hell of a lot shorter and lonelier for you.'

I didn't know what to say. I had tried so hard to be just like him, detached and inward that I had missed the fact it was all an act. I had always known that he loved us but in front of people he wouldn't show affection towards my Mum and me. I had always taken it as it would be a sign of weakness to let the outside World see you in that way.

'I've disappointed you, haven't I?' I said.

'Ruben, it's not about being disappointed or not. You're grown man now. I'm very proud of your independence but you are pushing everyone away. I've only ever wanted you to be happy, to start your own family and hopefully do a better job than you think I did.' I started to cry. I had always looked at him as this unapproachable and strong person to be respected. We hadn't had a meaningful conversation since I had become an adult. Maybe that was more my doing. He stood and crossed the small unplanted bed that separated us and pulled me to my feet. He was still strong. For the first time in years he hugged me.

'I meant open up a bit not cry in public like a little girl.' He laughed and put his hand on the back of my head and pulled me in to him. I sobbed and left a stain on his shoulder.

'Come on.' He said. 'Let's go, I'm starving, and your Mum will be waiting.'

CHAPTER 10.

I drove back North. Crossing under the Thames I tried to put Charlie out of my mind for a while. I would start looking for her in the morning. I thought about having a joint and a couple of beers. I'd have to stop to get the beers and a bottle of Whiskey. I could order a pizza.

I sat waiting for the lights to change so I could cross Upper Street when a girl caught my eye. She looked at me and smiled. I gave a half arsed wave and immediately regretted the action. She didn't wave back. She was beautiful. Natural. I watched while she said her goodbyes to the friends she was with. Probably not my kind of people, especially if they drank round here. They would be from the Home Counties and would have lived in a Market Town before finishing University and signing up with a French Bank or a Trading House. I didn't notice the lights change to green till a cyclist banged on my window and shouted something at me. I told him to fuck off and moved the old Golf on towards the Caledonian Road. As I drove past her, I took a quick look. She was laughing at something that a slimy, posh looking tit had said. He had his hand on the bottom of her back and boat shoes with no socks on. Definitely not my kind of someone. He was probably going to take her to an expensive restaurant and buy a bottle of Champagne, one I couldn't pronounce let alone afford. She looked at me again as I pulled level. She had a great smile. Tanned skin. Absolutely gorgeous. I could see them lazing beside a pool on Sardinia or one of the Greek Isles. He would bring her some fresh fruit and they would laugh at how rich he was and what great biceps he had. I thought about pulling over, but he noticed me slow down and looked across and noticed me staring so I carried on. What would I have said anyway?

There was no sign of Charlie back at the flat, so I put on the Led Zeppelin 3 CD and poured a drink. I stood at the breakfast bar and opened some post. The burn mark still bothered me. It was only a shit piece of laminate, but I would lose £600 at least. I looked at the walls in the flat. They were white once, now it was a mixture of nicotine yellow and browning from damp. The council didn't give these places a second thought. They were an expensive nuisance to them. As long as the rent was paid every month and there were no complaints or requests for refurbishments, they couldn't care who lived in them. That was all the landlord had said to me when I took the flat.

'Don't fuck it up and you can stay as long as you want.'

'I may only take it for a 6 month period to start with. I'll have to see how it works out for me.' I replied.

'I don't care. Just don't cause the Police to be called and don't have any parties. If you break something, replace it.'

'Is that it?'

'Make sure you pay on time every month or I will throw your stuff in the street and have a bonfire. It'll be your own private Guy Fawkes night.' He laughed. 'And don't give me reason to have come around here in the middle of the night. The old girl downstairs is friends with my Mum, and she is a nosey cunt, so I hear about everything that happens in this block.'

'Thanks.'

I offered my hand in a way of sealing the deal. He took it and squeezed too hard.

'Don't be a cunt.' He said and then left. Not the nicest of people and as I found out later a bona fide Right-wing holocaust denier.

CHAPTER 11.

Unfortunately, my Nan had succumbed to her non-existent illness, so I had managed to get the rest of the week as compassionate leave from work. Stuart couldn't have been more sympathetic. I wasn't happy about lying about the death of a family member especially my Nan, but I needed the time off.

I had decided to spend the week hunting down Charlie. How hard could it be to find her? I spent the day catching up on some reading and looking at maps of East London. I was reading "The Catcher in the Rye". Someone had been reading it in a coffee shop I passed on the way to work and I liked the cover.

I had got bored by lunchtime and gone to the bar. I asked Ryan if she had been in. He just laughed told me to pay my bar bill and walked away whistling.

The next day I jumped in the car and drove the few miles to the East. By the afternoon my detective skills had been exhausted. Walking around the Brick Lane area asking if anybody knows a Charlie only brings attention from the Police who thought I was mad. Maybe I was. Charlie was plainly fucking nuts and here I was trying to find her. I thought of going home, at least this way I get a clean break. Confused and hungry I bought myself a salt beef Bagel, sat in the car and ate it while I thought about my next move. The mustard made me thirsty. I routed through the glovebox and found a secret miniature bottle of Jameson. I had a quick look round to make sure the Police had moved on. Charlie had told me that since the terrorists had tried to kill everyone in New York this part of London had undercover Police hiding in every darkened doorway. Could have been one of her conspiracy's but I checked anyway.

I finished the bottle in one. There was a bang on the passenger window. I jumped and dropped the empty on the floor. Standing there staring through the window was a young Asian boy, probably about 18. I leant across and unwound the window.

'Sorry friend. You're parked across the access to our shop.' I looked past him and saw 3 others about the same age.

'No worries, give me a minute.' I said. I was just about to start the engine when I thought I'd ask the kid if he knew Charlie.

'Do you have a photo? We know most of the trendies round here.' He replied.

I dug the phone out of my pocket and found a photo taken a few weeks ago at the bar. 'She works round here. A clothes shop, I'm not sure of the name though.' I showed them the screen. 'She's the one on the right.'

The first kid looked at me. 'No shit mate. There's only you and her in the photo.' They looked at the phone for longer than I would of to be fair. One of them said something to the others in a language I didn't recognise, and they all started laughing.

'What's so funny?' They carried on laughing.

'Don't make me get out you little pricks.' I hoped they didn't make me get out. There was four of them and I'd never been much of a fighter. They stopped laughing and stared at me through the windows.

'Who is she to you? She isn't your sister, is she?' He looked sincere.

'She's sort of my girlfriend. Why?' I was a little worried.

'Shit. I'm sorry mate.' He rubbed his chin as if there was a beard growing. There wasn't.

'Will you tell me what the fuck is going on?' I shouted.

He turned and said something to the bigger one at the back

who replied in the same language that I didn't understand. They spoke loudly at each other for the next 30 seconds until I had had enough. I jumped out of the car and ran around the front squaring up to them.

'Unless someone starts speaking in English and tells me what has happened to her, we'll have business.'

'Calm yourself. You're in the wrong part of London to be throwing threats around.' The big one was right. It would be quite easy for these boys to give me a kicking and then dump me at the end of the road. I couldn't see many people would step in to stop it.

'Just tell me what you know. I haven't seen her for a while and I'm starting to worry.'

'One minute.' The first boy said.

They started talking between themselves. I lit a cigarette and blew the smoke directly into them hoping to speed things up. They all looked at me.

'Ok, before you start getting really aggressive and blow more smoke at us. Your sort of girlfriend is a local brass mate. Sort of.' I took my phone out and thrust the photo towards the four young men again. They were mistaken. I waived the phone around until the bigger one stepped forward and put his hand on my arm and took the phone.

'Listen mate. I don't know you and to be honest I don't want to, but you need to get out of here.' He threw my phone back through the car window.

'Wait.' I said. 'She told me she works for a clothes shop, so you've probably got her face mixed up with someone else's.' I was clutching at straws. I started mumbling to myself. 'You're just little boys with nothing better to do. You don't know her.' I swung a punch at the bigger one and caught him on the side of the head. The others grabbed me and pinned me to the car. It was a shit punch to be fair.

'You fucking idiot. I'm trying to help you. By rights I should cut you for that.' He pulled a knife from his jacket. I tensed my stomach waiting for the pain. Someone shouted something from across the road. They all let go at the same time.

'I know her because I've fucked her and paid for it.' He may as well of stuck that knife in. I felt sick. 'She belongs to an arsehole called Abdul. He's been putting the word about that he is looking for a stupid white boy called Ruben. He never gave a reason. I guess you are that stupid white boy.'

'But she' The words caught in my throat. I turned quickly and vomited down the side of my car. He put his hand under my arm and ushered me back to the driver's side. He opened the door and pushed me inside.

'Go back to where you're from and stay there. Don't go to any of the places you went with her.' My head was spinning. She couldn't have been a hooker.

'Why do you give a shit? You fucked her as well.'

'I don't care about you or her. I hate Abdul. He stabbed my cousin a few months back. I know that not being able to find you will hurt his pride and make him look weak.'

'I still need to make sure she's OK. Where can I find her?'

'Go home, get drunk and forget about her. Maybe next week you'll still be alive, maybe you won't. She'll be fine. Girls like her always are.' He slammed my door shut and the four of them walked away.

After ten minutes and two more miniatures I started the engine and pulled away. I headed South. I needed to get out of London. I would call an old friend who lived out in Kent. Hopefully I could stay there for a bit. I turned towards my Dads first.

CHAPTER 12.

The rain was coming down heavy when I pulled up outside the allotment gates. I could see my Dad still going about his business as if it was brilliant sunshine. I flashed my lights. Nothing. I flashed again. This time he looked up but shook his head and carried on pulling up a plant of some description. Realising he wasn't going to come to me I stepped out of the dry, comfortable car and ran across to my Dads patch.

'What are you doing Dad? Have you lost your mind?'

'It's just rain. I don't think anyone has died because of a bit of rain.'

'I think they have actually. At least you have a coat on this time.' I looked around the allotment. He was the only one out here.

'So, what do we owe the pleasure of another visit? Twice in a matter of days. You must have really made a balls up this time.' He said

'It's a bit my fault but not 100 percent this time.' I pushed the wet hair out of my face trying to think of the best way to tell him what was happening. It was still a shock to me. I had pulled over twice to be sick on the way.

'I take it it's this Charlie girl. Did you find her? Or maybe her husband found you.'

'Can we get out of the rain? I'm soaking.' I said.

'Pussy, let's go in to the shed. I have a good bottle of Whiskey in there. You can warm your little self up.'

Inside the shed were a couple of old wooden chairs, my Dads gardening tools and a hell of a lot of dust and spiders.

'When was the last time you had a clean-up in here?' I said looking inside an old jam jar he kept rusty screws in.

'Sit down and I'll pour us a drink.' I sat down on the healthier looking of the chairs.

'Mind if I smoke in here?' I said watching him measuring a single shot for me and a double for himself. Tight old fucker.

'Burst into flames for all I care. Just crack the door.' He had a chuckle at his joke. The same joke he had said a thousand times.

'So, either she was married, and the husband has found out or worse and she's pregnant.' He handed me the glass and sat down opposite me. I lit a cigarette and inhaled deeply.

'It's worse. If she was pregnant or married, I could deal with that. I have done in the past. But this, I just don't know.' He stood and grabbed the bottle from the dusty side. He filled my glass and sat back down.

'Turns out she was a prostitute.' I watched his face for a reaction. He sighed far too loudly, like he wasn't really listening.

'OK and how do you know this? Did you catch up with her?' He said.

'Not exactly. I walked the roads around Brick Lane asking people if they knew her. It's where she had told me she worked. I was having some lunch when a group of Asian blokes told me they recognised her photo. One of them had had sex with her.' The more I spoke about it the more the whole thing got to me.

'What did you have to eat?' He asked.

'Salt beef bagel.'

'Mustard and pickles?'

'Of course.' I replied.

'So, while you were doing your best Sherlock impression and

eating your lunch. You must be very worried about her by the way if you have time to stop for lunch. Some young Asian lads tells you that your girlfriend is a hooker?' He leant back in his chair and sipped his Whiskey looking out at the rain.

'Is that it?' I said. 'Anymore pearls to add?'

'No. Sorry I've got nothing.' He finished his glass and refilled us both.

'That's not where the problem ends though.'

'What else is there? Is she going to use your flat as a knocking shop?' He was still looking out of the window.

'She has a pimp who is now going to kill me if he can find me.' I flicked my cigarette through the crack in the door and lit another. I wanted to cry. If I wasn't sitting with my Dad I would have brought out the cocaine.

He looked at me, with a sudden look of panic on his face. 'Does she have this address? Does she know where your mother and me live?'

'No of course not, I only ever mentioned where I grew up. I never told her where you lived now.' I wasn't actually sure if I told her.

'Good so, what are you going to do? You obviously can't go home, and you are definitely not staying here. We have your "dying" Nan staying.'

'Thank you for the offer. Nan died by the way. That's how I got this week off. I'm gonna stay with Peter.'

'Peter?' His face went from panic to confused. I thought he may have been having a stroke. 'As in your former best friend Peter?'

'What do you mean former? Do you know if he's changed his number? I tried to call him on the way here, but it kept saying number not in use.' I flicked the cigarette out the door and let it close.

'You really live in your own World, don't you? For a start by former I mean you slept with his sister and then treated her like a stalker. When was the last time you called or spoke to him?'

'I spoke to him a little while ago to straighten all that mix up with his sister out. We cleared the air.' I said.

'When?' He asked.

'When what?'

'When did you last speak to him? I can guarantee it wasn't in the last 12 months.' He had a smug look.

'I spoke to him about 5 months ago. We were going to meet for a beer.'

'And he didn't mention that he had moved to Menorca with his new Wife? Or that he was expecting his first child?' I did not know any of this.

'He lives in Rochester. Why would he move to Majorca and not tell me?'

'Menorca. If you remember I was friends with his family long before you were born. I bumped into his uncle a few months back and he told me all about his wedding and new house. It has sea views.' I was shocked. 'Supposedly in a place called Es Castell. I looked it up. Looks lovely. Little harbour full of restaurants and bars.'

'What does he do out there? He worked in the City as a trader.'

'He's still a trader but he works for himself now. Don't ask me how.' I held my glass out for a refill and drank it before it had time to settle.

I tried to think of what to do. I had nowhere else to go. I had no one else. The only option I had was to go home and hide out for a few days till it blew over. I'd make a stop on this side of the water and get some supplies to last a week.

'You have money in the bank, don't you?' My Dad asked.

'Yeah, a bit, but I can't lend you any. I think I'm gonna need it.' I replied without thinking.

'You're an idiot. I don't want your money. I was going to suggest that you go home, pack a bag and get out of the country for a bit.'

'I'd lose my job. I'm already on my last warning. My boss turned up early the other week and caught me being sick out of the window.'

He shook his head. 'Or stay around London and wind up buried in the woods somewhere.' He stood and poured us both a drink. 'I don't want to have to identify your body Ruben. For all your faults, you are still my Son and I love you.'

It made sense to run. I could do with a break and there were always other jobs. To be fair I worked for a bunch of tits so it would do me a favour to be sacked.

'That's not a bad idea now you mention it. I could do with a break after losing my dear Nan.' I drained the glass and smiled at him.

'You're a little prick.' The rain had stopped outside. I gave my Dad an uncomfortable hug and left the shed. As I sat in the car watching him carrying on with his patch, I realised that I would never be the man he was. Then again, it was a different time now. People of my generation wasn't as interested in starting a family and having kids by the time they were in their mid-twenties as my Dads were. I started the car and pulled slowly away.

CHAPTER 13.

I headed back up the A2 towards the Blackwall Tunnel. I needed my Passport more than anything else. Buying more clothes could be done anywhere but to get a new Passport would take too long. I also needed my watch. It wasn't an expensive one, but it was all I had of my Grandfathers. I had always been promised his war medals when he died but had ended up with his watch instead. My cousin got the medals, so I was a little grateful that they weren't just sold off. As I came out of the tunnel, I realised that any Asian man could be this Abdul or one of his cronies. I didn't have a clue what he looked like. I stared at an old Sikh driving in the Toyota next to me. Obviously not Abdul but I was paranoid, so I put my foot down and moved away from him.

I pulled up a few streets away from the flat and sat in silence. It was dark. I'd have to get into the flat as quickly as I could. I looked around the inside of the car for a weapon, anything that could do a bit of damage. Nothing. I got out and walked towards Caledonian Road. As I got close to my building, I noticed a car parked just inside my street. It didn't belong around here. The only people who drove this class of Mercedes in this part of North London were either footballers who had got lost on the way back to Hertfordshire or Gangsters. I walked past, head down and into the off-licence a few doors down from my own. I nodded to the small old lady serving and poked my head out of the door. The car had blacked out windows so I couldn't see who was inside.

'Bottle of Jameson and a two pack of Marlboro please.' I said without taking my eyes off the car. The till rang into life.

'40 pounds.'

I turned to look at her. 'Prices gone up a bit, haven't they?' I said.

'You still owe from last time.' She replied.

'Shit.' I paid her the money and turned back to the door. I was being paranoid. Surely Charlie wouldn't have given my address to them. Maybe they beat it out of her. The thought made me feel sick. I put it out of my head and opened the bottle and had a swig. Two teenagers walked past the shop.

'Hey kids. You want to earn 20 pounds?'

'Fuck off you nonce.' One replied without looking.

'Serious come here.' I showed them the money. It got their attention.

'What do you want then? I'm not touching your dick.' The smaller more confident one said. He looked slightly malnourished.

'All I want you to do is give the back of that car a kick and run.' I pointed to the Mercedes.

'That's it?' They asked almost together. 'Who's in it?'

'I don't know yet. That's all you have to do.'

They sized up the car. 'Shit, I'd have done that for a tenner.' The little one said snatching the note from my hand. The other one whispered something to him and they both laughed.

'What did he say?' They had already turned before I had finished and broke into a jog towards the car.

I took an extra step inside the door so just the top of my head and eyes were visible. As they drew level with the car one of them took something from his coat and without breaking stride threw it straight through the back window. Almost as soon as the glass shattered the doors to the car flew open and 3

Asian men jumped out and chased the boys towards Richmond Avenue. I pulled up the collar on my Mac and slipped onto the street. I focused on the car and didn't look at anything else until I reached the door to my building. If anyone else came at me from the car I wanted to be ready. As I put the key in the lock, I looked in the direction the kids had run. They would never catch them, and if they did, they would wish they hadn't.

I sat in the living room and left the lights off. There was a streetlight just outside the window that gave enough light. I had used it a few times when I couldn't afford to put money on the electricity key. Sitting in the beaten up leather chair I had bought thinking I would redo the upholstery one day, I drank. I couldn't believe that she would give them my address. Maybe they tortured her for it. Maybe she had given it up quite happily. Either way I was fucked and wouldn't be able to come back for some time, if ever. I still didn't know where I was going to go.

My phone rang. I looked at the screen, it was Charlie. I dismissed the call and lit a cigarette. I regretted hanging up. She could have been calling for me to rescue her. I imagined myself running to my car and racing across town to save her from the pimp. The phone rang again, I answered it this time.

'You've got a nerve calling me. I have gangsters sitting outside the flat.' I was angry but if she said she loved me I would be putting my hero plan into action. 'Why didn't you tell me who or what you were?'

'I didn't have a choice Ruben. They kept asking me who I had been with. I don't know who told them about you in the first place.' She was crying.

'Where are you? I'm coming to get you. I don't care what they do to me.'

'Thank you, Ruben but I've already left. I can't tell you where in case they get you to talk. I'm going to call them in a few days to work out a deal, but I need to be as far away as I can first. You should leave as well.'

'I'm leaving in the morning. I just don't know where to go. I can't come back here for a while.'

'Just go anywhere that isn't there. Go back to South London he won't find you there. He's not allowed to go south of the river. Or go abroad.'

'Well I thought about Berlin. I remember the photo's you showed me before, it looked nice.'

'Yes, go to Berlin. Book your tickets tonight. There are lots of tourists there, so you'll be able to get lost.' She had stopped crying.

I put the cigarette out, stood and walked to the window. Police had arrived and were taking notes. A women officer was questioning the men who had been in the car. She looked quite hot. They obviously didn't catch the two boys.

'Charlie, I want to tell you that you're the first person that I think I was properly in love with. I'm sorry for sleeping with the other one.'

'Ruben, I think what I have done trumps your little indiscretion but thank you. Look after yourself.' I watched as the Police split the men up.

'Charlie do me a huge favour?'

'Anything.'

'Call the Police and tell them that you have seen some Asian men in a car on the corner of Stanmore Street and you think one of them had a gun.'

'Ok Ruben, for what it's worth I think I loved you as well. As frustrating as you are, you're the only person who wanted to spend time with me and not just have sex. You treated me like an actual person.' She hung up before I could respond.

I didn't know if I would ever speak to her let alone see her again. As I watched the Officers question the men, I prayed that she would be Ok. Not to God because let's be fair, he gave up on his wretched experiment a long time ago. I just prayed to myself.

I sat back down in the chair not knowing if she would call it through. I poured another drink and lit a cigarette. Maybe Berlin wouldn't be too bad, I could relax and sleep. Some sleep sounded good about now. I sipped the Whiskey letting the warm sensation relax my mind. After a few minutes I heard shouts from outside and jumped back to the window. The two Officers now had their batons in hand, one of the men was on the floor holding his head. The other two on their knees. She had made the call. I guessed or maybe they really did have guns. Soon the area would be covered in Anti-terror police and I would be able to walk out of here in the morning. Three Asian men suspected to be armed this close to Kings Cross Station. They would be lucky if they were out of prison before Christmas.

CHAPTER 14.

I woke with a start. Christ knows how long I had been out for. I had been dreaming of Charlie and me sitting on a beach, we were reading books and drinking Thai beer. I was reading John Fante, she was reading some shit Chic-lit. The sun was warming our faces and the sea was a crystal blue. We hadn't a care in the World. I've never believed Paradise was somewhere you could go. It couldn't be an actual place, or the World and their Mother would have fucked it by now. It had to be a state of mind. I didn't want the dream to end.

The morning sun had filled my living room with enough light to show the empty bottle of Jameson lying at my feet. I lifted the glass next to me and drained what was left. I checked my watch, it was 10.30am. My head felt like someone had put an axe through it. I reached down and picked up the Marlboro packet, took one out and lit it and stood. I tried to walk to the window but had a rush of blood to the head. Steadying myself on the breakfast bar I felt the sick in my throat and just made it to the sink before it exploded from my mouth. I didn't have time to move the plates. I ran the tap and washed the sick away and filled a glass with water and drank some.

I walked to the window and looked down to where the car from the night before had been. Armed Police had swarmed all over the men and the car. I didn't see if they had found anything, but the 3 men had been bungled into the back of an unmarked van and driven away. Poor fuckers, they were probably naked in a room somewhere in London being waterboarded until they give up the location of Bin Laden and his forty wives.

After the fun outside had died down I had turned the laptop on and booked a hotel in Rome, the flights weren't for another day so I could spend the hours tying up loose ends and then make my way to the Airport where I had booked another hotel for the night. I had taken a look at Berlin but the photos on the site made it appear a bit grey.

I rang Stuart first. I had to quit. I was on my last warning and another piece of unauthorised absence would be the end of my time there anyway. I pressed his name and his number rang.

'Ruben, how are you? I hope you're not thinking of coming back so soon. I did say take the week off.'

I almost felt bad. 'Stuart, I have a confession to make. You're really not going to like it though.'

'What do you mean?'

'My Nan isn't dead. In fact, she's not even ill. I told you that because I know that your own Nan had just died and that you were more likely to let me have the time off.'

'But how could you be so vile?' He sounded devastated.

'Don't be a twat, Stuart. I have a lot going on, so I won't be coming back. I'll post my work phone to you.'

'I'm sorry but I don't understand. Why are you leaving? You can't leave.'

'Don't be melodramatic. I never liked you. I didn't have a clue what I was doing most of the time and to top it off I fucked your cousin. I also know that you did too you sick bastard.' I was on a roll.

'Why are you saying these things? I think you may need to see someone; you're having some kind of breakdown.' He replied.

'Are you being intentionally retarded? I'm leaving. Tell Alysa I said goodbye.' I hung up.

I went into the bedroom and took the bag out from under the bed. I filled it with the usual clothes people take on holiday and threw my Passport on top. I was just about to close the wardrobe door when I noticed a small bag tucked under an old shirt of Charlie's. I took it out and sat on the bed. Inside was a good amount of Coke. I smiled. Who knows how long it had been there or when she had bought it? I opened the bag dug a coin in and sniffed a nice sized lump straight from the dirty twenty pence. It was good and it was coming to Rome. I laid back on the bed. The thought that she had made it away eased my mind. I did Love her in a strange dysfunctional way. Even if she was a prostitute who could still potentially get me killed. I took another hit of the Coke and got myself ready to leave.

CHAPTER 15.

It was just after one before I made it to Angel Tube so decided to go for some lunch before heading south. I hated the underground. Full of people who had no choice but to completely disregard somebody's personal space. I once had a woman cough directly into my mouth because the train was so busy, she couldn't hold on let alone lift her hand to cover her mouth. It was a disgusting way to have to travel. I had left the Golf with Nikoli to use till I got back.

I walked back up Upper street to look for somewhere to eat found a pub and went in. The place had the look of an establishment that had been spruced up quickly and cheaply to cater for the new breed of Islingtonions that had started moving to the area a few years ago. They came looking for a village feel but with the hint of danger and gangsters just around the corner.

The council estates are not as sprawling as they were in the South, but they are equally dangerous to people who don't know the etiquette. These people from the Home Counties thrived on mixing with the rough and downtrodden while they sipped Pinot and French Martini's in the new bars that had replaced the local corner pubs.

'Yes Sir?' The barman had designer stubble that he had spent far too long nurturing.

'What bottle beer do you have?' I asked.

He began quoting a list of brands I had never heard of. I stared passed his quiff to an old mirror that was hanging behind him. One of the few original items left from the makeover. I heard

Becks.

'That'll do.' I quickly said before he could move on. '2 bottles of Becks.'

'Certainly Sir. Good choice.' He turned to the fridge behind his arse and produced the cold, opened bottles before I could get my wallet out. I gave him a tenner and took a sip of the beer.

'Thank you.' He said. I drank the rest of the bottle in one and put the empty to one side. The barman returned with my change and handed it to me on a small silver dish.

'What's that?' I asked looking at the dish.

'Your change Sir.' I looked at him and then back at the dish. There were two twenty pence coins and a ten.

'Where's the rest? And why the stupid dish?'

'It's £4.75 a bottle. You gave me ten pounds that means fifty pence change.' I thought I'd miss heard. 'It does show the prices on the list over there.' He thumbed towards the end of the bar. I squinted but still couldn't see the numbers.

'Can I get you anything else?' He asked. 'Or there is another pub on the corner that has "deals" on bottled beer.'

'Do you sell food?'

'Kitchen doesn't open till 2pm.'

'Then no.' I didn't like him. Swaggering little prick. He walked away to the other side to serve a group of women who had just walked in. I hope they didn't expect food at lunchtime. I didn't pay attention to them.

I took longer over the second bottle. This was the reason why I avoided these types of drinking holes. Overpriced and no soul. It was all about how you looked, what brand of shoes you were wearing rather than the atmosphere. There were no proper fights between the regulars. The toilet doors had the top and bottoms cut off so the steroid freak bouncers could see you taking a shit without having to strain their oversized necks. The pretty boys took Ketamine rather than Cocaine these days. Where was the fun in feeling like you were stuck to a wall for three hours?

I looked at the mirror again. It was a fake antique, but it still looked nice. Probably all that was left from before the poor refurb'. The group of girls had started ordering drinks. I heard Pinot and switched off again. This time tomorrow I'd be in Rome and away from this City. I had enough money saved that I wouldn't have to worry for quite a few weeks. If I liked it, I could always sell the Golf and get a thousand at least for that. Thank God for the European Union. I could stay there for as long as I wanted without a visa.

I finished the second bottle and headed outside to smoke a cigarette. The barman asked something as I opened the door, I didn't turn to find out what. As I stepped onto the pavement the noise from the road hit me. I thought about moving out of London. It was too manic here. Too many people. I longed for a quieter place, somewhere more suburban. I opened the packet and took out a cigarette. I smoked two straight, lighting the second from the first. When I finished, I threw the butt on the floor and stepped back into the pub.

'I thought you had gone.' The barman said. 'I called you as you left but you must not have heard me.'

'No, I heard you. I just chose not to answer.' I replied. 'Why would I go and leave my bags?'

'Wouldn't be the strangest thing I've found left in here.' I finished the second bottle and pushed it in his direction.

'I'll have another. Then you can tell me what the strangest thing is.' He could be quite interesting after all I thought.

'Just the one?' He asked.

'Unless you're on commission, yes.'

He smirked and turned to the fridge. He put two bottles on the bar. 'Seconds on me. You look like you may need it.' Didn't know what he meant but I'd never turn down such a friendly gesture.

'Thanks. So, what is it?' His beard wasn't as stupid looking as I first thought. I liked the moustache. Made him look like a cowboy. I thought about growing one. I already had the beard.

'So, I found a baby in here once.' He said.

'Stop it. You're making that up. I'm not gonna stay here any longer just because you make up stories.'

'Seriously. 2 months ago, I came on shift and there was a pram in the corner, over there by the Fruit Machine.' He pointed and I turned, trying to imagine a pram and baby there. 'I walked over and pulled back the sheet and there it was. A baby no older than a few months fast asleep.'

I was enthralled now. 'What did you do?'

'Well someone came to the bar, so I went and served them, double Scotch. I kept an eye on the pram. I assumed that the parent had gone to the toilet or for a cigarette. It was quiet so I didn't see the harm.'

'You didn't see the harm in someone leaving a baby to go to the toilet? In a London pub.'

'Like I said it was quiet, there was probably only a handful of people in here and I knew most of them by first name.'

'Ok. So, then what? Did anyone come?'

'I watched the pram for half hour or so, but it started to get busier and I thought I better go for a smoke while I could.' I stared at him for a few seconds waiting for the rest of the sentence. Nothing. He just lent against the bar curling his whiskers.

'And?'

‘And when I came back the pram was gone. Suppose the parents realised they forgot their baby or something’ He opened the second bottle and slid it towards me.

‘You suppose? You didn’t check with anyone? The baby could have been sold to traffickers by now.’ I was livid.

‘Not my problem. Can you imagine the hassle if I’d have rung the Police? They’d have shut us down for the rest of the day.’

‘Well aren’t you a delightful person. I’m sure your parents are very proud of the well-rounded fucking piece of shit you have become.’ I wanted to break the bottle over his head.

‘Listen mate I just bought you a beer. Don’t get on your high horse with me or I’ll throw you out.’ He stood up straight to make himself look bigger. It worked.

‘Best thing for you to do is go to the other side of the bar before I put this bottle down your throat.’ He stepped forward. I clenched my fist around the neck of the bottle.

‘Excuse me, but when you two have finished measuring dicks can we get another round?’ I didn’t look in the direction of the voice. He turned first.

‘Finish your drink and fuck off you ungrateful arsehole.’ He said moving to far end of the bar where the group of women were.

I sipped my drink as slowly as I could. I wasn’t going to be pushed out by him. I was thinking of calling the Police and trying to explain about the child, but self-preservation got the better of me. If I was going to slip out of England unnoticed and without a knife in the back it was probably best, I didn’t get involved in a missing child. And for all I knew the parents could have been the ones who came back for the poor little bugger. I ordered another beer and a whiskey with the other barman. I didn’t get change from ten pounds.

I was nursing the whiskey but could feel someone close to me. I clenched my teeth waiting for the first blow.

'Hi, do we know each other?' I didn't look. It was a woman's voice, so I felt safe enough to keep staring at the glass.

'I doubt it.' I replied.

'You look familiar. Do you drink here a lot?'

'First time. Last time. You must have me confused with someone else.'

'Are you sure?'

'Quite sure.' I dropped my shoulder slightly. Short of telling her to go away I couldn't make it more obvious that I didn't want to talk.

'Maybe I've seen you shopping or something. Do you live round here?'

I turned to face her. 'Are you being obtuse on purpose? I'm not interested. I want to finish my drink in peace and leave. I don't know you.' I drained the last of my drink, slammed the glass on the bar and picked up my bags. The girl was standing opened mouthed. I walked past her and then stopped. It wasn't her fault my life had gone to shit. She was trying to be courteous, friendly. I turned to her again.

'Listen, I'm sorry. I just got some bad news today so I'm a bit snappy and the barman wound me up. I shouldn't have taken it out on you.' I looked at her properly this time and realised why she recognised me. 'You were on the corner with that bloke. You smiled at me.'

'I won't bother next time.' She walked back to her friends. One of them looked at me and sneered. She was ugly enough not to need to turn her nose up at people.

I didn't want to leave it this way, so I dropped my bag and walked across to where she was standing.

'Excuse me, can I have a quiet word please?' I tapped her arm.

Her ugly friend looked me up and down. 'Why don't you leave her alone and get out.' She looked even worse up close.

'Why don't you go out back and scare the rats away.' I laughed at my own joke. The gathering of women stared at me in disgust.

I looked at the girl. 'Please. It'll only take a minute.' I held out my hand. Not for her to take it but more to guide her away from the baying pack.

'What do you want?' She didn't move.

'I just wanted to apologise.'

'You already have. I won't lose any sleep so just leave.' She turned her back.

I walked back to my bag picked it up and left the pub. Outside I lit a cigarette and started walking back to the Underground. The Sun had come out, so I put my sunglasses on.

CHAPTER 16.

I had been in Rome for less than twenty four hours and had only left the small third floor room for a few hours to eat, buy a few of bottles of Whiskey and some cigarettes. The room itself was basic but had clean sheets, coffee making facilities and a good sized en-suite. It could have done with a lick of paint but the slightly worn greenish walls added a certain ambience. There was even a bedside reading lamp, which was nice.

I had managed to smuggle the half ounce of cocaine in so was pretty much set for the week. Other than flying with a weeklong hangover sitting next to a wailing child the whole way this was the most uncomfortable part of the journey. I'm not an international criminal and the chance of spending the better part my life behind bars in a dirty foreign prison being molested everyday isn't the most appealing of thoughts but sometimes even drug trafficking is a necessity to be able to leave the shit behind you.

The Hotel Trevi had been the first hotel I had found on the Internet. It claimed to have views of the Piazza Barbarini which I'm sure it did. My window looked directly onto the wall of the building to the side of the hotel. The porter who had shown me to the room the previous evening had said that I did indeed have the view but that you would have to slightly lean out of the window to see it. This was true if you didn't mind the fact that a slight lean out was an exaggeration and to see the Piazza would mean almost certain death on the cobbled road below.

I gave up trying to get a look at the Piazza and took the huge two steps back to the faded fabric armchairs and coffee table that offered the only seating area apart from the under whelming double bed. I sat down a took a long deep hit of Whiskey straight from the bottle, carved out a line of powder, rolled a twenty note and inhaled. I lit a Marlboro and leaned back waiting for the Whiskey and coke to run their course. Fuck the view I thought. I could just take a walk if I was that bothered. At least I wasn't being overlooked.

CHAPTER 17.

The lock to the bathroom snapped open and out she walked. Brown ringlet hair halfway down to her perfectly shaped arse, legs long enough to make any man's mind wander. Those eyes that had sucked me in the first time I had seen them. They were so dark you could get lost in them for hours. It could have been the drugs that gave her those eyes but either way they beckoned you in and took hold of your very soul.

'Why do you drink so much?' She asked while towelling her hair.

I tried to ignore the question. 8am was no time for this type of interrogation.

'Well? Why do you drink so much?' She was persistent. 'Are you trying to kill yourself, because there are quicker ways?' I had to think of a way to get this girl the fuck out of my room.

'Is that not a strange question coming from a prostitute' I replied.

'Why would it be a strange question just because I get paid for sex?' She sat down on the chair next to me, took the cigarette from my fingers and put it between her pouting lips. three hours ago, my dick had been where the Marlboro now sat. It had not been the quiet first night I had planned.

'Why do you care how much I drink? It's none of your business. I think you've forgotten how this works. I fuck you I pay you and then you leave.'

'Listen to me.' She shouted. 'We were having a good time last night before you realised what I am. I have to say I meet many fucked up men who have a lot of issues and you don't give off the same vibe as them. You still seem young enough to have a good life. You're not as damaged as you think' I cut her off. 'Aren't I paying you for sex? I didn't realise it came with a free head check as well.'

'Fuck you. I'm just trying to say the drinking and drugs are not the answer. Whatever you are trying to forget will still be there when you wake up. Get out of your own head for a minute.'

I cut in again. 'So how much do I owe you? I'm not paying for the analysis.' She looked straight at me with those beautiful eyes for a moment trying to work me out. She stood and moved back to bed without dignifying my question.

I sat and stared at the wet arse print her perfect shape had left on the fabric, I lit a cigarette and thought of all the arses that had been naked on that chair. It slightly repulsed me. I also thought about breakfast. It was too early for this kind of conversation and I certainly wasn't having it with someone who a few hours ago had let me do a line of coke off her stomach. No matter how beautiful she was.

'Have you been doing this kind of thing long?' I asked trying to lighten the mood. She looked at me, her breasts on show. They were unbelievably pert.

'A couple of years. I'm paying to get through college and raising my child.'

I raised my eyes 'Oh right.' I said.

'Cliché I know.'

'Why is it a cliché? Are we not all just following what someone has already done before us?' I said trying not to sound too much like a twat. 'Nobody has an original idea anymore. It would be impossible. Listen, I didn't mean to be rude before. It's been a hectic couple of weeks. Or months.'

'Is that why you're here?' She looked round the tired room. It was depressing the more I looked at it.

'Sort of. I needed a break, and the internet said how easy it was to get lost in Rome.'

I closed my eyes stubbing the cigarette out and tried to relax. It had been a while since I had properly slept. I could hear the girl talking but couldn't make out what she was saying. I hoped I wouldn't dream. If I drank enough then I never went off deep enough to dream. I was shocked with how easy the calmness came.

I woke with a start and jumped out of the chair; the girl had cleared out. I didn't know how long I had been asleep, but my head felt like it had been hours. I checked the coke, none missing. Found my wallet under the edge of the bed, she had taken what was owed to her plus a hundred Euro tip. She was good at her job but not worth that much. The head exam had wiped out any tip coming to her anyway. I searched the rest of my meagre travelling items and noticed the only other thing taken was one of the unopened bottles of Whiskey. At least she hadn't completely wiped me out.

I poured a small glass of Whiskey and put the drugs in the safe. I downed the drink and thought about what to do next. With only had a quarter bottle of whiskey left now I would have to go out soon which would mean facing hundreds of people. I smelled myself and decided to take a shower.

CHAPTER 18.

I had just pulled up my boxers when there was a knock on the door. I had a quick scan of the room to make sure nothing incriminating was on show and opened the door. Standing in the hallway was the Porter from the previous day. He looked sheepish and like he needed to take a piss at the same time.

'Can I help you?'

'Mr Humphrey, can I come in? I need to speak to you in private.' I pushed the door open and invited him in. He scurried past and double tapped to the window.

'It's Ruben by the way.'

'I'm sorry Mr Humphrey.' He was confused.

'My name is Ruben. I'm not keen on people calling me Mr Humphrey, it sounds too official and unless you've come to arrest me, I'd prefer to keep it personal. Now what can I help you with? I was just about to go out for breakfast.'

Now he was even more confused. 'Mr Humphrey as the Hotels Assistant Manager I am at liberty to inform you that Hotel Trevi does not allow guests to bring back certain types of women at night and that if this was to happen again the Hotel Manager will be forced to ask you to leave to Hotel.' He had started to sweat. The morning Sun had begun to rise above the buildings opposite and a warm beam of sunlight was burning into the back of his neck.

'Your English is very good. Where did you learn?'

'Pardon me? I don't.' More sweating.

'Your English. Have you lived in Britain or did you learn at school?'

'Oh, yes excuse me. I lived just outside London for 5 years while I worked for a restaurant there.'

'Well it's very good. You should be proud.' He ignored my clumsy attempts at flattery and carried on with the speech he had prepared.

'Those types of women sir, will not be allowed to stay here again.' I thought I was going to have to rehydrate the man. This was obviously the first time he had had to rebuke a guest.

'What if she was my cousin?'

'She wasn't your cousin Mr Humphrey.'

'Of course, she wasn't. I'm just asking as I may be meeting my cousin this week and could possibly want her to stay the night here. It would be silly for her to get a room when I already have one.'

He didn't speak for a few moments while he second guessed what his Managers response would be. I took the opportunity to light a cigarette and put the kettle on.

Finally, he had an answer, 'I suppose if she was a relative it would be OK but where would she sleep? You only have the one bed.' I think the boy was simple.

'I would sleep on the floor. You do supply extra bedding on request?'

'Of course, Mr Humphrey.' Satisfied that I had been properly dealt with he, bid me an enjoyable day in Rome, gave me some tips on where to eat and left me to my coffee.

I sat at the table and thought about the young woman I had defiled the night before. The question she had asked had begun to get to me. What was I running from really? It couldn't just have been about Charlie and her pimp. Every woman I had been with, I had in some way fucked over. I couldn't keep on the way I was going.

I didn't fall in love with every woman I met, I needed them. I could talk to a woman better than a man. I had grown up with only a handful of friends most of them I didn't particularly like. I'd learnt from an early age that boys couldn't be trusted. There was always an ulterior motive with them. They would try to be better than you, to steal from you, try to prove they were bigger and stronger. So, fuck them I would concentrate on the fairer sex. They looked better, smelt better and when I hit my teenage years the results of the friendships were a lot sweeter than anything some idiot with a football could offer.

I finished getting dressed and made another coffee. I smoked a cigarette and drank the coffee too quickly.

CHAPTER 19.

It was midday before I was finally ready to leave the Hotel. After the Assistant Manager had left, I had had another few drinks and knocked through a couple of lines. Not the greatest start to a day but not the worst. I made my way down the stairs, crossed the reception and said hello to who I assumed to be the Manager before walking out onto the now busy Via Sistina. I looked back through the doors and saw the Manager had taken a position in the middle of the marble tiled floor. He gave off the impression that my indiscreet tryst the night before was a personal affront to his position not only as a Hotel Manager but also as a Father. I thought maybe he had a Daughter who was a bit loose too. With enough drugs in my safe to put me away for a good few years I couldn't take the risk of him calling in the local Police to search my room. I decided to head back in to try and make amends, after all I had brought a hooker to his Hotel so it was the least I could do.

I stepped back into the cool reception. 'Can I help you Mr Humphrey?' Stern voice, he definitely wasn't a fan.

'I just wanted to apologise for last night. The lady I brought back.'

He cut in 'Was a prostitute Mr Humphrey.' It sounded disgusting the way he said it.

'No, there must be a mistake. She wasn't a prostitute. I meet her in a bar down by the Trevi Fountain.' I don't know why I was bothering to try and defend myself. He knew what she was, I knew what she was.

'Mr Humphrey please don't insult me. I have been a Manager of many hotels in Rome for the past twenty years. I know the vast majority of these girls by first name. I have known most of their Mothers too.'

'Right, well I just wanted to say sorry for any ill-feelings I may have caused.' I went to turn and leave when he held my arm. I looked at his hand on my arm and then at his face.

'There are certain rules that you will stick to should you wish to bring one of these women here again.'

'Being?' I asked. I wasn't about to be told what I could and couldn't do by some jumped up bellboy.

'Mr Humphrey should you choose to organise your own acquaintance and not go through myself you will have to pay a...' He paused while an elderly couple passed us.

He continued. 'I think the English term is corkage.'

'Corkage. That's a rather emotionless way of putting it.'

'Mr Humphrey let me try to explain. Would you go to a restaurant and take your own wine and expect not to have to pay for that privilege? No, you would not, and the same rule applies here. You can fuck whoever you want but one way or another if you are paying for it you will be paying me also. Good day Mr Humphrey and don't forget to see the Spanish steps. They are beautiful in the Autumn.' He turned and walked away.

'It's Ruben by the way.' It was all I could come back with. He turned and faced me again.

'Good day Mr Humphrey.' He smiled and walked behind the oak reception desk. I couldn't leave it like that, so I followed him. The elderly couple were at the desk asking the Assistant Manager the quickest way to the Pantheon, so I had to wait my turn. The Manager looked at me and then back to the screen hidden from view. This was his Castle and I would have to wait till he was ready to speak to me. The old couple were going through every leaflet the Hotel had. I couldn't wait all day, so I stepped to the side and directly in front of the Manager.

'Sorry I didn't quite catch your name before.' I looked at the old couple and smiled. I think they were Canadian.

'My apologies Mr Humphrey. My name is Antonio but please call me Toni.'

'Thank you, Antonio. As we were discussing before, if I were to bring my own wine back to the Hotel. Do I need to ask your permission first or see you when I get back with the wine?'

'Mr Humphrey that would be entirely your decision but either way Hotel policy is that you pay corkage on alcohol that is not purchased through ourselves. I'm sorry.' The old lady had started to listen in to our conversation. She placed her hand on my forearm. I couldn't understand why people kept touching me.

'Excuse me.' She said. 'I don't mean to butt in but do you not like the wine they serve here? I've found it to be better than most Hotels.'

'It's not that I don't like their wine. I haven't tried it. My argument is that sometimes I find you could have been out and had a lovely day sightseeing, you walk past a window when a bottle catches your eye.'

'Mr Humphrey, I must insist.' Antonio tried to interrupt. I raised my hand to stop him.

I carried on. 'A bottle catches your eye. It's all you can do not to drink it right there on the street like a hobo. You tell yourself not to be greedy. You rush back to your room to savour the delights of that bottle. So, I'm saying you can't plan when a good bottle of wine will snatch you from your daydream.' The old lady took her hand from my arm and patted the back of my hand. She smiled and reminded me of my own Nan.

'You sound like you have such a passion for wine my dear. Antonio I must insist you wave this young man's charge. It is not often you see the younger generation interested in the finer things.'

She put her had on my face. I thought of Charlie and almost hugged the old girl and cry. If only we weren't really talking about prostitutes this would have been a very sincere moment.

'I'll see what I can do Mrs O'Connor.' Antonio said. I caught a glimpse of him, his jaw was clenched.

CHAPTER 20.

'Mr Humphrey, we haven't seen you for a couple of days.' After the corkage conversation I had done my best to avoid Antonio and his rat assistant Luca. I had even gone as far as climbing down the fire escape at the back of the building and walking through a restaurant kitchen just to get out of having to walk past these two pimps.

'I've be exploring your beautiful city. So much to see and not enough time to see it.' While not climbing down the side of buildings I had actually been visiting some of the sites. The city was amazing. Everywhere you looked there was some sort of historical building or ancient remains. It was the most normal I had felt in while and it was a good feeling.

'That's good to hear. A quiet word if you will Mr Humphrey.'

'I think we have moved passed the need to be formal, don't you? Please call me Ruben.'

'As you ask Ruben. We have the small matter of settling the bill for your little indiscretion two nights ago.'

'I thought you were going to waive that?'

'Why did you think that? Ruben as I have said before if you choose to supply your own entertainment there is a charge. Today that charge is fifty Euros.'

'And If I refuse to pay?' I could see he was trying to keep his cool.

'Mr Humphrey if you choose not to pay, I will be forced to call the Police and have them search your room. I'm sure they will not go easy on a drug smuggler with a substantial amount of cocaine in his safe.' He had me by the balls. I looked at Luca, I knew it had been him in my room routing through my bags and safe. I thought about my options for a few seconds. I had none.

'Fine, fifty Euros it is.' I said trying to sound as indifferent to them as possible.

'Another thing that I will need you to do Ruben.' He said.

'Back to Ruben, are we?' I replied.

'As you are obviously a lonely traveller, I request that you have company for this evening.'

'I'm fine, thanks for the concern though. I'm not that lonely anyway.' Luca was grinning behind his master.

'I must insist Ruben. Rome is a wonderful city and to have a beautiful girl on your arm. You can't imagine how the city transforms when you are with a lover.'

'How much will this cost me?' I was being hustled by this slimy arsehole. He could charge me whatever he wanted and there was nothing I could do about it.

'Not as much as the two hundred and fifty Euros the last one took from you.' He smiled. 'The fee for tonight's entertainment is one hundred Euros for the girl and my seventy five Euros for providing the service. Quite fair I think.' Again, that fucking smile.

'Fair for who? Not me. I've got to pay hundred and seventy five Euros for something I don't want or need plus an extra fifty Euros.' What he said before suddenly hit me. 'How do you know how much I paid? What did you take from Ioana?' It dawned on me that this thieving sadist would never have let her leave the Hotel without paying her due's.

'I'll make you a deal Ruben. I waive the fifty Euros you owe me, and you take the girl tonight with no more arguments.'

'It's not really a deal is it? I don't have a choice.'

'No, you don't.' Luca smiled at me. I wanted to stick a pen in his eye.

'Ok shall we say 7pm in my room.' I wasn't happy but there was nothing more I could do.

'Of course. Would you like me to book you a table somewhere?'

'I'd like you to fuck off and die.'

'I'll take that as a no. Good day Ruben, I'll make the necessary arrangements for tonight.'

I left the Hotel and turned towards the Piazza and the Metro station. I wanted to forget what had just happened and needed a drink so walked past the Metro to the restaurant on the corner. I ordered a bottle of beer and a double whiskey on the side. The waiter took a sly look at his watch.

'Yes, I know it's 10am thank you. Just get the drinks.' I snapped probably a bit too loudly. A couple on the table next to me shot a glance and muttered something in French. I ignored them and went outside for a smoke.

The drinks helped me calm down about the ridiculous situation I was in. I couldn't believe I'd come here to clear my head and get some peace a quiet and now found myself in more trouble than if I'd stayed in London.

I ordered another whiskey and closed my eyes enjoying the mid-morning sun warming my face. In October Rome was still warm enough to sit outside with a small jacket on. I sat listening to the music being played by the restaurant. It was some kind of classical piano. I had never been one for that type of music but at this moment it seemed to be the only type of music I should be listening to.

The waiter came back with my drink.

'What is this playing?' I asked.

'Chopin, Sir. It bothers you. I can turn it down.'

‘No, please it’s relaxing. I’ve just never heard it before.’ He left me to my drink. I sat and closed my eyes again; God I was tired. I’d always been into 60’s and 70’s music. The Stones, Zepplin, Jimmy Hendrix, Canned Heat. Not really music you can doze off to. This on the other hand was exactly what I needed right now. I made a mental note to search out this Chopin when I got back. It sounded like a Sunday afternoon sitting in a quiet bar kind of album.

I considered my next move. I would have to pay for the girl but I didn’t have to fuck her. I could try and keep some form of morality in this whole sordid business. I would also change Hotels tomorrow for the last few of days of my stay. I knew Antonio took the evening off between 5pm and 7pm so I would sneak out then. I lit a cigarette and downed my drink feeling like I had made some head way. I ordered another double and a bottle of beer on the side. I had made a plan so thought it only right to celebrate.

‘Your first time in Rome Sir?’ The waiter was back quicker this time. Obviously hoping for a tip.

‘Yes. Beautiful city.’

‘On your own?’ He placed the drinks down and started wiping down the table next to me and looking suspicious.

‘Yes, I’m just looking to relax and get lost in the crowds to be honest.’

‘OK sir, Rome is the perfect place for that kind of thing. If you need anything, advice on where to go or anything else please feel free to ask.’ He gave me a not so subtle wink.

‘What are you talking about?’ I would punch this fucker in the face if he offered to set me up.

‘Sorry Sir but you struck me as someone who may be on the lookout for some smoke or blow.’ He had a quick double take that no one was within ear shot. This was great news. I had enough coke, but some weed would be good to relax with and get some sleep.

'Fantastic, can you get some weed? I really need to chill out for a bit, you know?'

'Of course, twenty Euros and I'll get you some very good weed.'

'I don't want it now though. I'll come past in a few hours and pick it up. And stop calling me Sir.'

'Ok. Where are you staying, I could always drop it off to you?' I've always been a bit cautious of telling people where I'm staying when abroad. Especially when it concerns drugs, but he gave off a genuine vibe. Someone trying to supplement his not so life changing salary.

'Hotel Trevi. Just around the corner.' His face changed from happy to what the fuck in a blink of an eye.

'Best you meet me here then. Signor Antonio would not be happy to see me in his hotel.'

'Fuck him, you would be my guest.'

'You do not understand, Signor Antonio is a very well connected man and very dangerous himself. I wouldn't be allowed inside the doors unless I were a paying guest.' He was visibly scared.

'Ok I'll meet you here in a few hours. Can you get me some papers as well?'

'Of course. I'm Marco by the way.'

'Thanks Marco. Ruben.' I shook his hand and stubbed out the cigarette. 'So, where's best to get lost in this place.' I said.

'The Colosseum. Thousands of tourists all looking for the same photo's. Keep a hand on your wallet though, lots of Romanian pickpocket gangs there.' He smiled and walked away to a table of Korean tourists who were frantically photographing everything and anything that moved or looked remotely older than a loaf of bread. They had already photographed each other while eating a dozen or so times. Every time with a different expression on their faces.

I stood and left the bill money and a good tip under the ashtray. I needed to be among normal people. People who weren't being bribed by the local Mafioso into paying for prostitutes or drug dealing waiters.

I walked back to the Metro station, bought a ticket and stepped onto the escalator. I always wanted to see the Colosseum. I couldn't think of a better place to be lost for a few hours.

CHAPTER 21.

'Excuse me, do you speak English?' I half turned hoping that it wasn't me they had asked and someone else was stood behind me.

'A little.' I said, attempting humour and failing. She smiled. Nice teeth.

'Funny.' She replied. 'Do you know how I get to the Colosseum?' She was American, not my normal type, not just because she was American, but quite attractive. Had a strange piercing in her cheek.

'That's where I'm heading.' I said without thinking. I was transfixed by her cheek piercing.

'No shit? Would you mind if I tagged along? I don't want to get lost.'

'Yeah of course.' I said. I Couldn't really have said no fuck off I'm actually trying to spend some quality time on my own.

'Great. I've been stood at the entrance for 20 minutes asking people if they could help me. I couldn't work out how to get there.' We reached the bottom of the escalator. I stepped off.

'Why didn't you look at the map?'

'I did but it's in Italian. Do you speak Italian?' We walked onto the platform.

'No, but the it said Colleseo on the map so I'm taking a punt that that is the Colosseum.' I couldn't work out if this girl was stupid of naive. I'd read somewhere that a huge percentage of Americans didn't own a passport and that some had never even left their own state. Maybe this was her first time abroad I thought.

She laughed. 'Oh my God, you must think I'm stupid?'

I did. 'Erm. Stupid would be a bit strong.' I laughed as I said it trying to make it into a joke. The train pulled into the station. 'Like you say you don't speak Italian.'

We bundled on to the train. Not as busy as the Central line but enough people to mean I was very close to the face of the American. Smelt like she had drunk a lot of coffee that morning. She had nice perfume though, floral and fresh.

'I'm Lauren by the way.' She said far too loud.

'Ruben.' I replied offering a very English gentlemanly handshake. The train jerked and my hand landed fully on her left breast. As I pulled my hand back there was a small unintentional squeeze.

'Embarrassing when that happens isn't it?' She said seeming not the slightest bit fazed by the mild groping that had just occurred. I was blushing.

'Sorry about that. Shit I didn't mean to. It was the train.'

'Ruben, calm down. You're sounding very British.' I didn't know what to say next. A good few minutes went by before all I could muster was a garbled question about how long she had been in Rome. She laughed and rubbed the side of my arm.

The train pulled into the Colleseo station. We got off. I was still uncomfortable about grabbing her tits. 'Listen, again I'm sorry for what happened. The train jerked and my hand was already out there. I'm not a deviant. I'm not going to bundle you into a Taxi.' She put her hand on my arm again to shut me up.

'Ruben, seriously I'm not bothered. I grew up in LA and after years of taking the bus there I don't consider it assault unless a piece of you is inside me.' She laughed. A cool but slightly odd way of seeing things. 'And anyway, there is always time for that later.' She added.

'Los Angeles. I've always wanted to go there.' I felt better that she was ok with a bit of groping every now and again and looking at her as we walked out of the station, I thought she was better looking than I had first decided and may also be up for some light foreplay.

'Wow, will you look at that.' She said. I turned my head and saw the Colosseum for the first time.

'Fuck me that's impressive.' I wasn't joking. Around two thousand years old and the thing was still standing strong. I had worked on buildings that hadn't lasted ten years before being ripped down.

'Is that all you've got?' She said. 'Some of the most progressive architecture the ancient world has given us and all you can muster is "Fuck me, that's impressive".'

I shrugged. 'Let's find somewhere to eat.' She laughed and followed me as I tried to find somewhere that wasn't going to rip me off for being a tourist next to the biggest attraction in Rome.

We sat at a table facing the Colosseum. I browsed the menu everything was six or seven Euros more expensive than it should have been.

'See anything you like?' She said without looking up.

'Not really. Think I'll just get some fries and a drink.'

'So, I take it you're not a foodie then?'

'Look around you. Most of the people here couldn't give two shits about what they're eating. It's all about where they are. 90 percent of the food served here is probably precooked out by the airport and then heated up in a microwave.'

'Jesus, anyone ever told you to lighten up a bit?' She said. 'Enjoy the moment.'

'A few times. I'm just saying I doubt you'll find Haute Cuisine here. Their kitchen probably consists of 4 microwaves, a deep fat fryer and a handful of Albanians pushing the buttons.' She looked at me for a few seconds trying to work out if I was being serious, then went back to studying the menu. The waiter came over.

'Yes Madam?' He said. I could see her stressing over what to choose.

'Can we have, two lots of French Fries and I'll have a Coke to drink please.' The waiter sniffed his disapproval. I laughed.

'I'll have a double Scotch. Where are the toilets?' He pointed his pen towards the back.

'Excuse me. I'll be one minute. I need to piss.' I said as I pushed myself to my feet.

'Ok thanks for the heads up.' She replied. 'Actually, I'll have a beer instead of the Coke please.' The waiter made the change on his pad. I smiled and walked to the back of the restaurant. As I passed the kitchen, I poked my head through the open door. It was very clean and looked as though everything was being cooked from fresh. I couldn't see a microwave. I opened the door to the small toilet, stepped in and locked the door behind me. I took the beer mat I had taken off the bar as I passed out of my pocket and poured out a small heap of powder rolled a note and inhaled not bothering to sweep the drugs into lines.

Walking back past the kitchen and took another look, there was still nothing being deep fat fried and everyone seemed to be talking in Italian. As I made my way back to the table, I could see Lauren reading a guidebook to Rome. I would have to lose her after lunch.

I sat down and took a sip of the Scotch. It tasted like spiced dishwater. I spat it back into the glass.

'Something wrong with your drink?' She said still reading the guide.

'Tastes like shitty water.' I said smelling the glass.

'So, send it back then.' She replied laughing at the expression I had on my face.

'I'll wait till the food arrives. I reckon that waiter will spit on the chips if I say anything yet.'

'Why would he do that just because you don't like your drink?'

I shrugged. 'Because he might be an arsehole.' She shook her head in disbelief.

'I still can't understand you Brits. You'll quite happily finish and pay for that drink rather than send it back. You know the waiter probably doesn't care if you think the Whisky is shit or not. He'll get paid whatever happens.' She was laughing again. I'd definitely have to get rid of her.

'I honestly couldn't care less whether he would be offended by me sending the drink back. I just don't want one of my chips to end up entering the pot boys arse crack before I eat it.' I took another sip, it wasn't as bad as the first. Maybe I'd judged to early.

'You're very strange.' She said taking a sip of her beer. I wish I had ordered a bottle of beer as well. She looked at the glass. 'If you keep drinking it there'll be nothing left to send back.' I put the glass down. Lauren went back to her guide.

'Would you like to visit St Peter's Basilica with me after here? The book says it's a fantastic experience even if you are not a religious person.' I couldn't have thought of a worse place to visit. Just another Church but on a bigger scale.

'Would you mind putting that away?' I nodded towards the guidebook. She turned the book over and for some reason looked at the back cover.

'The book?' She replied.

'Yes, the book.' I said.

'Why?' She asked.

'Because it's a beacon to any robbers. It's the same as walking around with a thousand pound camera hanging round your neck. It marks you as a tourist.'

'Wow, that would be a heavy camera.' She smiled, closed the book and put it on the table. Not a bad joke I thought.

'Do you not think that our accents give us away as tourists?' She said.

The waiter came over and threw the two plates of fries on the table.

'Enjoy your food.' He said begrudgingly.

'Thanks. Can my friend change his drink please? It doesn't taste right.' The waiter looked at my glass then at me with a look that said "Where are your balls? Why can't you speak for yourself?"

'Yeah sorry, it tastes like the bottle has been open a while.' I quickly added.

'But Sir you have drunk half the glass already.'

'Thirsty.' I said. He picked up the glass. He was pissed off. I was glad I had waited for the food to be put down first.

'What would you like instead?'

'Do you have any Bourbon?'

'I'll bring you the drinks menu.' He stomped off towards the bar.

Lauren was picking at her fries while taking photos of the Colosseum across the busy road. I watched her for a minute not wanting to disturb her. She looked like she actually enjoyed being here amongst all these people. It made my skin crawl. I was starting to think that getting lost surrounded by so many people was the wrong idea. I should have just gone back to the room and climbed inside a bottle. I was just about to make my excuses when the waiter came back with the menu.

'The menu Sir.' He almost gave me a paper cut he shoved it into my hand so forcefully. I gave it a quick once over.

'You have Woodford Reserve?' I said almost shocked. 'Of course, sir.'

'Ok, I'll have a double Woodford please.' I said, quite pleased.

'Good choice sir.' He turned and walked away. He would probably spit in it. I would have done.

'That wasn't too difficult was it? Feel better?' Lauren said taking a photo of an old Italian women waiting to cross the road. Strange photo to take I thought. I ignored her and ate some chips. They were nice. Homemade. I didn't speak to her again until I had finished eating. I had always hated people trying to strike a conversation up while I was eating. Always felt like people were just trying to fill the uncomfortable silence. I liked the silence.

'So, what did you mean earlier when you said you still can't understand us Brits? How many do you know?' I said once I'd eaten the last chip. She put her fork down and drank some beer to clean the bits of chips from her teeth before speaking. It had always been a mystery to me why Americans were so obsessed with their teeth but didn't mind being the obesity country of the world. I suppose it's important to have gleaming white teeth while you're having your first stroke at 35 years old.

'Sorry did I not say before? I live in London. I'm studying drama there.' She finally said.

'Ok where abouts?'

'RADA actually.' She said it like I should have been impressed by the name.

'That's great. Firstly, I don't know what that means. And B. I meant where in London do you live?'

'Have you never heard of The Royal Academy of Dramatic Art? How have you never come across it before?' She was obviously shocked.

'Not something I would ever have been interested in.' I replied.

‘Sounds somewhere the rich and posh people go.’

‘Ok it’s basically one of the oldest and most prestigious acting schools in the world.’ She seemed very proud.

‘Congratulations on that. Where do you live in London?’ She looked slightly annoyed that I didn’t care that she went to acting school.

‘Hackney. Near the Burberry outlet, I share an apartment with a couple of other students.’ I knew the area. I drove through there on the way back home when I had been south of the water. Complete shit hole. Full of people trying too hard to be trendy and avoid being robbed or people who couldn’t understand why anyone would choose to live somewhere so awful.

‘Nice.’ I said. ‘Very up and coming.’

CHAPTER 22.

I finished the last of the Bourbon and was about to order another when the waiter put the bill down. 'I didn't ask for that.' I said. He ignored me and walked away.

'I'll get this. After all I drank more than you.'

'It's fine I'll pay my half.' She replied.

'Seriously I'd like to. It's been nice to have some company.' I took my wallet out to show that I wasn't bartering anymore.

'OK, but I'll take care of the tip.'

'Deal.' I replied.

She opened her purse and got out fifteen Euros and placed them on top of the sixty three I had put down. I waited for her to walk away and slipped the fifteen into my pocket. I'd never normally leave a tip. Especially for a couple of bowls of chips and below poor service. Nobody tips the people who work in McDonalds. I followed her to the street.

'So, what do you want to do now?' I asked. She pointed her thumb towards to the Colosseum.

'I thought
we could pop in there.' Sarcastic. I was beginning to like the girl more.

The Colosseum as a whole was quite interesting. I wouldn't say I'd rush to go back if I'm honest though. I found trying to spot the cats that live inside the Colosseum more exciting than the building itself. The whole place from the actors dressed as Centurions outside to the building itself needed a good wash.

'So, what do you think?' She said, reading one of the many signs that were placed around the walls.

'It's alright. Thought it would have been a bit more.' I couldn't think of anything it could have been a bit more of. 'You know.'

'Not really, no. I think they were going to put up some giant screens showing films but decided against it.'

'That would probably keep you inside for more than the ten minutes it should take me to walk round here.'

'How can you not be impressed? It was built two thousand years ago, and you can almost see the Gladiators in the ring down there, fighting for their lives.' She stood leaning against a barrier that lead to a huge fall to the basement area. The sign she had been reading said something about where the Gladiators would have prepared for battle. I caught a glimpse of a cat. That was 6 I thought. She looked pissed off.

'So, what does interest you? What do you do for a career?' She was persevering. I should have told her not to bother but I had a few hours to kill and didn't want to spend them on my own.

'I'm in construction. I build tiny apartments for already rich men so they can charge poor unfortunate souls between 5 and 10 times what they cost to build them. They get richer and I remain the same.'

'So, this place should amaze you then if you are into construction?' She wasn't getting it.

'I never said I was interested in it. It's just a job. It's something that I have to do to pay the bills. If I'm honest I despise the whole fucking industry.'

'If you are being honest then you must realise the people buying those places aren't that poor or unfortunate. If they can afford the obscene prices of London, then why should you care. Like you say it's just a job, you aren't saving lives. You strike me as somebody that doesn't want to be happy.' I wanted to push her over the barrier.

'So, after a couple of hours you have me all figured out. Well done. If I had known that you would have been such an intrusive bitch, I'd have ignored you like everyone else did.'

'Don't raise your voice at me.' She snapped. I hadn't realised I had. 'You miserable prick. I'm just trying to be polite and find out a little bit more about the person I've just had lunch with. If you don't want to talk say so and I'll go?'

I took a step towards her. 'Who are you talking you? Don't stand there trying to tell me how I don't want to be happy. You know nothing about me and maybe I don't want you to know anything about me.' She didn't reply. She just stared at me. I realised that there was no more than a few inches between us. I considered kissing her. She put a hand on my chest and pushed me back to arm's length.

I looked around. A few people had stopped and were watching to see if she'd slap me. I hoped that she wouldn't. I wanted to sit her down and tell that my life was a wreck and that secretly I'd like to jump off the top of this shitty old building.

'I think I'm going to leave. It's been nice up until now, but I think you need time to yourself. To sort out whatever shit you have going on. It's not my problem sorry.' She raised her hand to the side of my face and leant in and kissed me gently on the cheek. She held her soft, gentle lips there for longer than necessary. When she turned and walked away, I wanted to scream that I was sorry. That I hadn't meant any of it. I was lonely and needed someone to help stop the voices. I opened my mouth, but nothing came out. I watched her walk to the steps. She disappeared from view without looking back.

CHAPTER 23.

I left the Colosseum after half an hour. After Lauren had left me, walking around and counting cats on my own just seemed stupid and slightly sad. As I made my way outside, I saw some more ruins across the road so crossed to have a look. I overheard someone mention Nero and Palace, but I couldn't tell if they were talking about this place or one of the other thousand piles of stones in the area. I'd lost interest in the whole thing so looped back around and headed to the Metro station. I didn't have too long to wait for the weed so thought I'd just hit a couple of bars before I had to meet Marco.

Coming out of the Metro into the Piazza Barbarini I turned right away from the restaurant. I had an hour so walked towards the Trevi Fountain. Other than the sheer volume of tourists trying to throw a couple of cents into the pool and hoping to get that perfect shot just as the coins were in mid-air, the fountain is one of my favourite parts of Rome.

The Albert pub was close by and had a good few corners to hide up in for a while. I pushed the door open and approached the bar. The girl who had been working the night I had met Ioana, the prostitute from the first night, smiled at me and opened a bottle of beer before I could open my mouth. I thanked her, picked up the bottle and walked to the back of the pub. The place was empty so finding a table on my own was no trouble. Sitting at one of the old tables I sipped the cold beer and closed my eyes. I was exhausted. The weed would help. I had always managed to sleep well after a few joints. As long as I was allowed to.

I reached into my pocket and pulled out a copy of the "The

Sun Also Rises". I'd never been a huge fan of Hemmingway growing up, but Charlie had loved his novels and had always been on at me about trying to finish reading one of his books. I turned to the front page again. Charlie had scrawled "Just read it, you arse." I smiled. I read the first chapter, closed the book and set it to one side. Not that I didn't like it this time, but it reminded me of Charlie. I fished a copy of short stories by Charles Bukowski from my bag and put it on top of the Hemmingway book. I had got onto Charles Bukowski by accident as a teenager and loved his novels and short stories from the off. It was another disappointment that he was already dead by the time I'd discovered him. Like most of the bands that I listened to who had split up or died before I was even thought about. I had read almost all of his work and there would come a day when there wouldn't be anymore.

I took a long drink of the beer and tried not to think about the poor girl who I was supposed to be meeting in a few hours' time. I considered writing Charlie a letter. I'd never actually post it. I didn't know where to post it to. I'd read that writing your feelings and problems down on paper was a better form of therapy than anything you could pay for. Maybe I would, later.

I picked up the book and concentrated on a story I had started earlier. Two men had just broken into a house in an upmarket part of Los Angeles. I thought of Lauren, she was a nice girl. I shouldn't have let it end the way it had. I put the book down. They were just about to rape the owner's wife in the story. I sipped the beer and closed my eyes again reaching into my coat pocket for my cigarettes.

'You don't like Hemmingway or Bukowski? I have a book by a children's author if you like.' The girl from the bar had come to clean the tables. I hadn't noticed her walk over. She was pretty. Short hair that gave her an elfish look. She had an old Cream t-shirt on and ripped jeans.

'I like Bukowski but could never get into Hemmingway.' I replied.

She sat down opposite me. 'Why not? He was a genius.'

'I'm not sure why. Maybe it was the whole "Lost Generation" thing. Or the old way of speaking. I've never managed to get more than a few chapters into anything by F. Scott Fitzgerald either.'

'So, you haven't read Gatsby then?' She appeared shocked.

'Nope. Never have and never will. I tried one of his about Paradise or something. Got bored around twenty pages in.'

'You should, read all of them I mean. Ignore the idea that you have about them and just read their work as if you have never heard of either author.'

'You sound like an expert.'

'No, not really. I just think it's pointless reading a book with an impression of what you think it should be instead of just letting yourself be absorbed by the story. Also try to let the style and way they speak become the way you think. If only for the time you are reading.'

She stood and walked back to the bar. Some tourists had intruded on our conversation. She served them and came back to the table with two fresh beers. She sat down.

'Did you know that Hemmingway said you should write a story with the pencil first and then type it?' She said taking a mouthful of beer.

'I did not. Very interesting though.'

She picked up his book. 'So how far have you got with this one?' She flicked to the middle.

'First chapter.'

'So, you didn't like it this time because you didn't like it before or because someone told you they didn't like it?'

'The opposite actually. It was Ok but it reminds me of someone who loved it.'

'I'm sorry.' She said putting the book down. 'Do you mind me asking if that's why you are here in Rome? You drink like you are trying to forget someone or get over their passing.'

'There not dead. Just gone.'

'Oh.' She sipped her beer looking for the right thing to say next. 'Could be worse.'

'How's that?'

'Who knows.' She smiled. 'Try the book again. Hemmingway never really agreed with the Lost Generation either.' She finished the beer. I loved a woman who could drink beer. Or whiskey. A woman sitting in bar with a whiskey blew my fragile mind.

'Maybe I will then.' I said. 'So how do you know so much about all this?'

'Because I read. Listen to your friend and just read it. You arse.'

'Fair enough.'

She stood and left the table. I finished my drink and put the books back in my bag and went outside for a cigarette. The bargirl was busy serving a couple of Americans who wanted to order food as well. She didn't notice me leaving. I thought about going back to the hotel, packing my stuff and getting the hell out of Dodge and heading back to London. It had been a shit trip to be honest. I had come to Rome to get away from prostitutes and on the first night had ended up in bed with one. Now I was being extorted by a pimp hotel manager and every woman I came into contact with thought I was a degenerate.

Back inside the bar I ordered a whiskey and sat down. It was the first time I had noticed a huge painting of Prince Albert, Queen Victoria's husband, hanging on the wall. I pulled the Hemmingway book back out and opened it. Maybe they were right, and I was just being an idiot. She looked over and smiled at me. I'd have to ask her name.

'So, what do think?' She tapped the spine of the book with an empty bottle.

'Not bad.' I replied.

'An understatement, no? You haven't looked up for forty-five minutes.'

'Maybe.' I said. 'By the way what's your name?'

CHAPTER 24.

I looked around the tiny courtyard. I hadn't even had a chance to order a drink before I had been grabbed by the arm and ushered through the kitchens and dumped out here.

'That's a nice way to treat customers.'

'Sorry Ruben but Signor Antonio is in the toilets. He's picking up his monthly tax.'

'I'm just having a drink in a local bar for fucks sake.'

'Trust me, it's better this way.'

He looked terrified. 'So why tell me to come at this time?'

'He's early. Just give me ten minutes. I'll get one of the porters to bring you a drink.'

'Ok. Make it a double.' The door had already closed.

I had finished the bottle of water a young kitchen porter had brought me and was kicking the empty around before Marco opened the door again. 'I'm very sorry Ruben he wouldn't leave.'

'No worries, thanks for the water. Had you run out of beer or whiskey?'

'I don't understand.' He replied handing me a small packet of green substance. I opened it and inhaled the smell. It stunk. Good sign.

'Cheers. Do you have any papers?' I passed him the money.

He pulled a packet of Rizala from his back pocket and tossed them at me. 'You'll have to leave via the back.' He thumbed towards an old doorway that must have led to the street.

‘You should have told me to use that way in the first place. At least you wouldn’t be all sweaty and clammy now.’

‘Thanks for the money.’ He said, then pointed to the doorway turned and went back inside.

I decided to hang around a bit. It was quite nice to be in this little yard. Nobody wanted anything from me here. It was quiet and away from the tourist cameras. I found an old oil tin. One of those huge ones that you see and can’t believe that they make olive oil in that size cans. Turning it upside down I rolled a joint and looked up at the windows that surrounded the courtyard. I thought about how the smell of the restaurant must drive the residents insane after a while.

When I was around sixteen, I had an evening job in an up-market pub kitchen washing pots and pans. I fucking hated it. The smell of the grease gets into your hair and your skin. It wouldn’t matter how much I scrubbed I could still smell it. One time I was leaving, and the Manager ask me if I could do her a favour. She was stunning so stupidly I agreed. She took me to the men’s toilet and ushered me inside. Some drunken bum had slipped while taking a piss and split his head open on the basin. It looked like a crime scene in there. The blood was splattered up the walls and had already started to congeal and mix with the urine in the corners. ‘If you can clean this up, I’ll pay you an extra hour’s money.’ She had said. ‘Ok.’ I replied. She handed me some gloves and left. I spent the next two hours picking up bits of bloodied jelly. It’s the only smell that took longer to get out of my nostrils than grease. I still can’t look at blood without having to sit down.

I finished rolling the joint, never my strongest talent, and lit up. I inhaled as much as I could hold before it felt as though my lungs would burst through my ribs. It was good strong weed and cleared the blood thoughts instantaneously. I sat and smoked half the joint before stubbing it out and poking it down inside my cigarette packet. I looked at my watch. About an hour before

I had to meet my "date". I sat and stared at the watch. My Grandad would have been spinning in his grave at the way my life had turned out. He would then probably laugh, clap and rub his hands together while tutting and raising his eyes to the kitchen ceiling.

I stood and walked out of the back door and made two rights towards the Via Sistina and started a very slow walk back to the hotel. I was a lot more stoned than I had hoped to be, but it felt good.

CHAPTER 25.

Pushing open the door to the hotel reception, I turned to flick a cigarette butt to the kerb and stepped into the cool, lobby. I stood for a second with my eyes shut so they could adjust to dim lights inside.

'Mr Humphrey, a good day sightseeing I hope?'

He must have been lurking behind the large pot plant that I didn't know the name of. When I opened my eyes, he was in front of me with a sadistic smile across his face.

'Yeah, thanks. I went to the Colosseum.' I replied and walked past him.

'And you liked? Such a beautiful piece of architecture.'

'I've seen better to be honest.' I didn't turn back to see him standing in the middle of his kingdom. Master of all he could see or fuck.

I made my way to lifts and got in the first one that came. I pressed the button to the 3rd floor. I could hear his shoes on the marble floor heading in my direction. He had a distinctive walk. Almost sounded like he had one leg shorter than the other. I pressed the button again, with a little more haste. His hand appeared in the void before the doors had had a chance to close. I hated these old, slow elevators.

'What?' I said.

'Mr Humphrey, I trust your meeting my friend will still be going ahead as planned tonight? It would be a terrible shame to let such a beauty down.'

'Do I have much of a choice.' I said.

'We are all free to make choices that will affect our lives.'

'Then no. The "meeting" is off.' I made the quotation signs with my fingers and instantly hated myself for it.

He winked at me and laughed. 'Very good Mr Humphrey. She will be with you in 30 minutes.' He reached passed my hand that was still hovering over the 3rd floor button and pressed the one with the close door sign on. He turned and walked away. I listened to his shoes with the Blakey's cross the floor as the doors closed.

I inhaled the two lines of cocaine straight after one another and downed the glass of whiskey I had poured. The cocaine burned the inside of my nose while the whiskey made me wince. I sat back in the chair and lit a cigarette. I looked at my watch, 15 minutes till my date arrived. I stood and paced to the bathroom then turned, walked back and sat down. Taking a deep pull on the cigarette I thought of Charlie. I wondered if she had made it to Scotland, I would go up there when I went home and try to find her. A proper goodbye. Maybe we could make it work. I could forget about her career choice. Scotland wasn't that big, and they only had a few big cities to search. I took a swig from the bottle and stubbed out the cigarette half smoked.

I finished what was left in the bottle and reached down to my rucksack for the one I had bought earlier.

Whiskey drinking had happened by chance. While on holiday in Tunisia the hotel that I was unfortunate enough to be staying in didn't know how to clean the pipes for the beer taps. The beer therefor tasted like sewage and the only other thing I recognised was a bottle of VAT 69 scotch whisky. I'd read somewhere that Hitler and Himmler used to drink it. Probably not true but drinking it you can almost see the weird little fuckers plotting the end of an entire race over a glass of blended scotch. After 10 days of drinking only whisky I was hooked.

I dabbed my finger in the cocaine and rubbed it around the inside of mouth, then put the bag in the safe. I didn't want the hooker finding it. I poured a large glass of whiskey and checked my watch again. Five past. She was late, and I'd wasted 20 minutes daydreaming. I downed the drink and went into the toilet, bending over the basin I splashed water on my face and caught my reflection in the mirror, it was the first time I had looked at myself in days. I looked gaunt and grey. The drinking was taking its toll. I made a deal there and then that it had to stop. Or at least calm down for a while. Dying had never really bothered me too much but I wanted to be a bit older than I am now. Pulling the light cord next to the mirror I went back into the bedroom and sat down.

I had a few more nights till my flight home. If I could make it through tonight, I'd change hotels, pour the coke down the toilet and start being a bit more normal. I honestly believed it was possible. I realised that I was biting my fingernails and stopped.

The knock on the door came 20 minutes later. I hated tardiness. Even if you are going to be slightly unprepared, still be on time. I took my time lighting a fresh cigarette and rose slowly from the chair. Taking the 3 strides to the door I peeked through the rusting spyhole, no sign of any beautiful young ladies. I opened the door.

'Mr Humphrey, Signor Antonio has asked me to inform you that your date for the evening will not be coming. She has been held up at…' I slammed the door without letting him finish the sentence.

I took the cocaine from the safe and poured three quarters of what was left on to the table. Not so much to last for a long weekend but enough. Stripping to my boxers I sat down taking a long drink from the bottle of whiskey. I was of course slightly relieved but at the same time hugely pissed off. The whole thing had been a way to show me he was in charge and could fuck me anytime he wanted to. I picked up the straw I had cut down earlier and bent over the pile of white powder inhaling around the edges and slumped down in the chair. I took a pull of the cigarette and held in for as long as possible until I could feel the burning in my lungs. Scanning the room, I felt the tears well in my eyes. I swallowed the emotions. This was the last place I wanted to open that black box.

I placed the spare bottle of whiskey I had and the cigarettes I could reach on the table and started drinking and inhaling with complete disregard. I must have drifted into some sort of catatonic state as the next thing I knew one of the bottles was empty, the cigarettes too. My nose and body felt like I'd been in a battle. I felt my shorts, they were soaking. I'd pissed myself at some point in. It could have been worse. I tried to stand but my head was spinning and I my brain wouldn't send the signals to my legs. I fell forward on to the bed. I couldn't move. As much as I tried, my legs wouldn't work. I managed to drag myself until my head was almost on the pillows. The inside of my head was on fire. For a moment I desperately tried to remember the advice about having a stroke. Then a sense of calm overtook me. As I stared into a strange brownish stain on the quilt cover, I thought, fuck it. If this was how I was going to go out, lying face down on a grubby bed wearing a pair of pissed stained pants and surrounded by drugs and empty bottles then so be it. It would be a bit disheartening for my parents, but they could make up a story. And at least I wouldn't be forced the indignity of having someone wiping my arse when I'm old.

I pulled the cigarette packet from the side table and an ashtray. I lit the joint I had smoked outside the restaurant. It would make dying easier. I took a few deep pulls and tossed the stub into the glass dish. I closed my eyes and waited for the inevitability of death to come with all its glory. The replay of my life wouldn't take long.

CHAPTER 26.

I opened my eyes to see Antonio and Laruen standing over me. For a moment I couldn't believe that even in the afterlife this prick was there. It was good to see Lauren again though. She had a pretty face.

'Mr Humphrey, good to see you in the world of the living.' My eyes went from his to Laurens and then back again. 'If it wasn't for your friend's insistence for me to open the door.' He tutted. 'That would have been an awkward phone call to the Police.'

'Get the fuck out.' At least I wasn't dead then.

'Ruben.' Lauren said.

'It is fine. Under the circumstances I think we can afford Mr Humphrey to lose his manners. But please do not speak to a lady in that way again.'

'You know I was only talking to you. Just get out.' I wiped the dribble away from the corner of my mouth and tried to push myself up. I slumped into the pillow. I ached all over.

'Ruben, what have you been taking? You look awful.'

'Has he left yet?' I murmured from deep in the pillow. It stank of mould.

'Sorry but would you mind leaving us please?' She said, her voice was sweet and caring.

'Of course. Mr Humphrey, I do hope you feel better soon.' He left and closed the door.

I rolled on to my back and reached for the cigarette pack.

'Can you pour me a drink please?' I said. My throat was on fire.

She picked up a glass and walked into the bathroom. She appeared a few moments later holding a glass of water.

'What the fucks that? I can't drink that. Foreign water makes you ill.'

She pulled the cigarette from my mouth took a long pull and stubbed it out. 'Drink the water and pull your shit together.'

'That was a waste.' I said. 'Why are you here anyway? And how did you find where I was staying?'

I wriggled my way up, so I was resting the back of neck on the headboard. I sipped the water, it tasted of iron, so I lit another cigarette to mask the taste.

'You mentioned you were staying on Via Sistina. I just went into the hotels and asked the reception if they had an obnoxious, alcoholic Englishman staying in the hotel.'

'So how did you find me then?' I smiled.

'You were actually the second Englishman of that description staying around here. Can you believe that in the hotel next door is an even more unpleasant moron?'

'I can. Rome seems to attract the worst sort of people. It's like London but with better pizza.' I blew a trail of blue smoke towards the peeling patch of plaster on the ceiling.

'So, what did you take then? The manager was worried that you had OD'd. How long had you been out?' She continued.

'He was worried he wouldn't get paid is all.' I checked my watch and realised that I had only actually been unconscious for around twenty minutes. Slightly embarrassing. In fact doing a quick piece of maths in my head the whole event had only lasted around an hour.

'I have no idea how long I was out. You didn't say why you were here.'

'I didn't want to leave it the way we had.' She sat on the arse print chair. She fitted into the print nicely.

'We only just met, like you said. So why does it matter how it was left?' I've left things with people I've known for years a lot worse.

She leant forward and took a cigarette out of the box at the bottom of the bed. She didn't light it.

'You may be a self-centred prick but I'm not. You have a lot of issues.'

'Obviously.' I cut in looking at the urine stain on my pants.

I found half a bottle of whiskey just under the side of the bed, opened it and threw the cap on the floor.

'I didn't want to leave being one of those issues.'

'Why do you give a fuck? I've known you for a few hours and you could have left and gone back to your little privileged life pretending to be an actress in London living amongst the poor people and acting cool.'

'You really are a sad arsehole, aren't you? I'm trying to tell you that I like you. For all your very obvious defects I think you could be a nice guy. I can feel it.'

'You can feel it can you?' I took a hit of the whiskey and a pull of the cigarette.

'Yeah I have a knack for that type of thing. And I wasn't raised to leave someone in trouble.'

She twirled the unlit cigarette between her fingers. I laughed, a little louder than I meant to.

'What's funny?' She said.

'So, are you psychic or something?'

'Not psychic, but my Mum and Dad brought me up in a commune in the hills outside LA. We were taught how to channel into people's auras, how to help them.'

I laughed out loud this time.

'How could I have guessed that you wouldn't believe in this type of stuff?'

'It's total bollocks. There are no such things as auras or healing powers or anything else.' I paused and looked at her. She was upset. I could tell that this meant a lot to her. 'I'm sorry. I don't want to upset you. You seem like a really nice person and you're obviously caring but I've never believed any of that stuff.'

She twirled the cigarette again. I smoked mine.

'It's fine. A lot of people refuse to accept it.'

'Are you going to smoke that?' I said.

'No.'

'How long since you gave up?'

'That was the first bit of a cigarette I've had in three months.'

'Congrats.' I said. 'You may not have guessed but I have that effect on people.'

'What effect?'

'Make them want to do things that will eventually kill them.'

She laughed. 'You know, talking helps. You can really get to the underlying problem by sharing your thoughts. You just need to open up.'

I pushed myself up a bit higher and put the cigarette out.

'Why are you Americans so obsessed with counselling and sharing your thoughts and deepest desires? It's a bit weird. I've never got my head around how you become the most powerful country in the world when you spend all your time crying that no one likes you.'

'That's just a cliché. We don't all go counselling. Most Americans can't afford it. Crack is cheaper. Don't forget we haven't got the Nanny State handing out bandages every time we fall over or get into money troubles like you Brits.'

She grabbed the lighter, lit up and inhaled deeper than I thought possible. There was that desire people had to end their life quicker after a brief time around me.

'Welcome back.' I said gesturing towards the white stick in her mouth. I put the bottle to my lips and drank.

'That's constructive.' She said.

'It makes me feel better.' I said taking another swig. More for effect this time.

'How? Honestly. How can being drunk or stoned all the time help?'

'You wouldn't understand.'

'Cut the shit Ruben.' She jumped to her feet and walked straight at me. I coward and she snatched the bottle from my hand and took a long swig herself.

'Don't go mad. That's the only bottle I have left.'

'Fuck you Ruben. You need to grow up and realise that it isn't always about you. There are a lot of people out there that have it a lot harder than you. You're a spoilt little shit.' She took another long swig. 'What was it? Did Mummy not love you enough? Was you not allowed the puppy when you were a kid?' She was getting warmed up now.

I took the bottle back and had a nip before she polished it off.

'Sorry to disappoint but it's none of the above. I genuinely do just enjoy being drunk and taking narcotics to make me forget about the wider World. There's no real mystery. I didn't have an Uncle that made surprise visits when my parents were at work. I am just a prick.'

She sat back down. Picking the cigarette up out of the ashtray she took short puffs and stared at me. I became a little nervous. I didn't do small talk, but I hated silences more.

'So, you like Whiskey?' I said. 'You know the Irish added the "e" in Whiskey?'

'What the fuck are you talking about?'

'The "e". The Scottish spell it w-h-i-s-k-y. No "e". Supposedly the Irish added it so you could tell the difference between the two or something like that.'

'And the fact one will have an Irish name and one a Scottish. And the fact of I don't fucking care.'

'Just thought it was interesting. You Americans do it too.'

'Do what?'

'Spell it with an "e".'

'Why are you in Rome?' She asked ignoring my last comment.

'What do you mean?'

'You're not here for the architecture or the history. I think we can definitely rule out the food.' She tossed the cigarette butt into the ashtray.

'Honestly?'

'For once would be nice.'

'It was the first City that came up when I typed in quick city breaks. I was going to go to Berlin, but Rome popped up.'

'Are you fucking kidding me? The last few hours of my trip of a lifetime are being ruined because you were too lazy to scroll down the page?'

'Ruined sounds a bit melodramatic, I thought we had some fun. But essentially, yes.'

'You cunt.'

I was slightly taken aback by her response. Five minutes ago, she wanted to save my soul and now I was a cunt. Americans don't say the word cunt enough in my opinion. I've never seen a problem with the word. There's no difference to calling someone a prick.

'I'm sorry. I didn't set out to ruin your trip. Jesus I'd never even met you until the yesterday. I've had a really bad couple of weeks and needed to get out of London quickly.'

'Why?' She lit another Marlboro. I felt bad, three months down the drain.

'The same reason as all the other lonely souls trying to get lost in a foreign city.'

'Go on'

'Boy meets girl, Girl goes nuts and turns out to be a prostitute. Pimp threatens to kill boy.' I exhaled hard to hammer home my angst.

'And?' She said.

'And what? That's it.'

'What happened to the girl? Did you love her?'

She reached across the bed for the bottle. I handed it to her.

'Bit personal. She fucked off to Scotland and left me to it. What else is there to say? She was a prostitute.'

'Are you really that self-absorbed? What do you mean "she left you to it?". What do you think the Pimp would have done to her before she managed to get away?' She took a hit from the bottle. 'Did you love her?'

I pulled what was left of the joint from the ashtray and lit it. I stared at the arse print chair and tried to blow smoke towards it. The fumes were sucked out of the window.

'She gave them my address. A whole team were waiting for me. I could have been killed.'

'Stop being such a fucking child Ruben. How the hell do you think they made her tell them? They probably beat her senseless.'

I took another pull of the joint and swapped it for the bottle and a plain cigarette. I'd never stopped to think about how scared Charlie might been having a gun shoved in her face. Not properly. I just wanted to get myself away. I didn't like the way this woman was able to get inside my head.

'Well? You haven't spoken in about five minutes Ruben, so you must have feelings for her.'

'I thought I loved her before she went mad. On Saturdays we used to drive south of the Thames and visit Greenwich park. We'd park up by the Observatory and walk over to the flower gardens and sit under a willow tree and have a picnic. We could lay there all day talking about nothing. Did you know they have deer in the park?'

'So why didn't you fight for her? She hadn't gone mad she just sounded very alone and frightened.'

'It would never have worked. It's not like we could have had a normal life with wedding bells and children.'

I tried flicking the cigarette butt into the ashtray and missed. Lauren picked it up and stubbed it out.

'You need to find her Ruben. You'll always regret it if you don't. Scotland isn't that big a place is it?'

'I can't. I asked her where in Scotland she was the last time I spoke to her. She told me it was for the best that we never see each other again. I had to make a promise to her.'

'Would you not be curious?'

'About what?'

'About whether it could work?' She motioned for the bottle. I passed it

'Not really. Maybe I did love her, but I love my own life more.'

She laughed swigging out of the bottle. 'So, you really are that shallow after all.'

'I really am, I thought I told you that. I have never met anyone who would make me feel like I would die for them. Other than my parents. And even then, I'd have to think it through before making a final decision.'

I took another swig and lit a cigarette. 'So, when do you leave? Rome, I mean. Not the room.'

'Tomorrow. You?'

'Not sure. I was going to leave in a few days, but I don't have a lot going on at home.'

We spent the rest of the night sat on the bed discussing our hopes and dreams. Mainly hers as I was already living the dream. I had called down to reception for a tray of cold beers and a bottle of whiskey. Antonio reminded me of the stay over charge for guests in a lovely written note that accompanied the tray. I set fire to the paper and threw it in the bathroom sink. I had every intention of leaving without paying the final bill anyway. I had used a stolen credit card to book the room and paid cash when I checked in and they hadn't asked for the credit card. I guess he wanted as much off the books as possible. My plan was to simply chuck my bags off the back terrace and use the fire exit. A traditional back door shuffle.

At around 1am Lauren stood suddenly and stubbed the cigarette out she had moments ago been enjoying.

'I need a taxi. I still have to pack for tomorrow.' She slurred.

I made a grab for her hand and missed. 'Stay.' I said.

'I don't think so. My flight is at midday, so I need some sleep before I leave for the airport.'

'So, miss the flight and I'll get you another one.' She leant over and cupped my cheek in her hand.

'That wouldn't be a good idea.' She replied. 'It's been a very odd experience meeting you Ruben. When you get home stay off the drink and drugs.' She kissed me gently on the forehead. 'You're a good person I think, you'll meet a nice girl who'll make you feel safe.'

She straightened and made a half stumble to the door.

‘Wait.’ I said. ‘You didn’t give me your address in London.’

‘Didn’t I?’ She closed the door behind her.

I started laughing draining the last of my beer. I soon realised the laughing had turned to tears. I was lonely and sat in a hotel room in a foreign country wearing piss stained pants surrounded by nothing but empty bottles and half smoked cigarettes. I wiped my eyes and mouth and lit a Marlboro. Blowing a thin line of blue smoke towards the yellow ceiling I thought of Charlie. I didn’t miss her so much as I missed someone caring for me. I was a selfish prick, I knew that.

I walked to the window and looked down to Via Sistina. It had started raining. I watched as Lauren climbed into the back seat of a taxi. She didn’t look up. I opened the window all the way and held my hands out to catch the rain. When they were almost full, I splash the rain on my face. It was probably cleaner than what would come from the tap in the bathroom. I left the window open to clear the smoke from the air changed my boxer shorts and fell onto the bed and dozed. I would jump ship tomorrow and head back to London.

CHAPTER 27.

'Mr Humphrey, you look well this morning. Considering last evening events, I was not expecting to see you so early. I trust you slept comfortably?'

'Yes, very refreshed. Thank you.'

Antonio moved from behind his desk before I could make the exit. I had already dropped my bags out of the back window into the courtyard of the neighbouring apartments. I wanted him to think I was going for breakfast. That way I'd estimated at least lunch time before he checked the room. The hotel had no direct access to the courtyard, but it would be easy enough to go through the apartment building. He moved in front of me blocking my escape.

'Mr Humphrey, your stay ends with us tomorrow. We normally ask all guests to settle accounts the day before they leave us.'

'Really, why's that?' I replied trying to move past.

'Would you like to settle now or when you return from breakfast?'

'Well to be honest, I've had such a great time since I arrived that I was going to enquire about staying longer. Do you have availability?'

'No, my apologies but we are already at capacity.' I looked around the reception, it was 10am and not a soul. In fact, I had only come across a few people since I'd checked in.

'From tomorrow.' He countered before I could speak again.

'Shame.' I thought for a second. 'Could you give me a printout or some sort of bill of what I owe. I'll go to the bank after I buy cigarettes.'

'Certainly Mr Humphrey. If you care to follow me to the desk.'

'Obviously you won't be able to add the "extras" so just scribble them on the bottom.' I said

'Don't worry, we have very expensive room service charges. Sometimes I can't believe our guests are willing to pay the costs.' He look at me and smiled. 'We can change travellers cheques here if you would prefer not to walk around with all that cash.'

'No, it's fine at the Bank. I'm sure they'll have a better exchange rate.' I replied.

He folded the printout from the copier and slid it across the desk. I tried to take it, but he didn't let go. He just held it and stared at me. 'Do you need directions to the nearest Bank?'

I took a travel guide from my pocket and held it up. 'No thank you, I'll find it.' I pulled the paper away and turned from the desk. As I pushed through the doors, I heard him move behind me.

'Ruben.'

'What?' I faced him.

'You didn't look at the final bill. How do you know it's correct?'

'What would the final number matter? I have to pay regardless of what it says.'

The prick smiled. 'You have learnt well Mr Humphrey. I will see you soon.'

I stepped on to the pavement and turned right. I knew he was watching me and that I now had five minutes at best before my room was checked. As soon as I thought I was out of eyesight I ran and slipped into the building in front of the courtyard. I didn't stop to look round I picked up my bags and ran back to the entrance. I had a good look in the direction of the hotel and then using a group of Asian's as cover I walked along and turned down Via Zucchelli. Before grabbing a Taxi for the airport, I threw the printout into the kerb without checking the amount.

The radio was playing "You can't always get what you want". I tapped the driver on the shoulder and asked him to turn it up. He shrugged and carried on talking into the phone pressed against his ear. I rolled the window down lit a cigarette and sank back into the seat. I'd be back in London in a few hours

CHAPTER 28.

I waited for my bag to come through the little black door at the end of the carousel. The belt hadn't started moving yet. Not that that stopped me and dozens of others jostling for position around the edge all in the vain hope that our bags will be first out. I pulled a miniature from my pocket and sank it. The belt lurched into life. I'm sure the middle aged man next to me came a little in his pants at the sight that his bag was first. I couldn't look him in the eye.

'First time that's ever happened.' He proudly announced to everyone in ear shot. Hopefully he'd end up having an impromptu prostrate examination by customs.

I collected my bag and made my way through the nothing to declare side. I had called Nikoli from the airport in Rome and asked him to pick me up. He agreed for £50. He was standing amongst the Taxi drivers and kidnappers holding a board with my name misspelt on.

'Good trip?' He asked.

'Nope.' I replied. 'And you've spelt my name wrong.'

'I was meant to. You're a wanted man still.' He threw the card on the floor and we made our way in the direction of the carpark.

As I settled into the passenger seat of his beaten Mercedes, he handed me a joint. 'Thanks.' I said lighting up without thinking.

'Careful. It has cocaine in.'

I took a few puffs and passed it to Nikoli. 'Did you manage to get passed the flat?'

'Yes a few times. No sign of any Muslim fanatics.' He laughed. 'I did do some digging around. He's a serious fucker this Abdul.' He passed the joint back. I didn't really want it. 'How much money can you raise at short notice?'

I turned to him. 'Why?'

'Six thousand makes the problem go away.'

I sat up. 'How's that?'

'I know someone who knows someone else. They spoke to this Abdul.'

'So, I give him the six grand and he doesn't kill me, and Charlie gets left alone?'

'Not exactly. You give me the money; I give it to my friend he takes his cut I take mine and the rest goes to Abdul. What happens to Charlie, I don't know? Hopefully she stays hidden. From what I can gather he still pissed that she ran. And of course, that you had his men arrested. They're still not out you know.'

'Why do you and your friend take a cut? How much does he actually want?'

He snatched the joint back took a long pull and threw the butt out the window. 'I'm taking five hundred for making the arrangement and my friend is taking five hundred for fuel and expenses.'

'Fuel and expenses? Fuck me, he's only going to East London, is he taking a helicopter?'

'Or you can make the delivery yourself and see what happens.' He smiled and swerved around a slow moving lorry.

'I can get you the money when we get back. What made him agree to the pay off?'

'He's a businessman at the end of the day. He keeps all of your Charlie's earnings for the last month and gets an extra five grand from you. Plus, supposedly she was a pain in his arse so it's a win win for him. By tomorrow morning this will all seem like a nightmare.'

'Seem like a bad dream, you mean?' I replied.

'What?'

'Nothing.' I lit a cigarette and settled back into the seat closing my eyes. Six thousand was a lot of money and would almost totally wipe out any savings I had. Better than losing my life though. 'Did you bring anything to drink?'

'Glovebox.' Nikoli had lit another cocaine joint. I cracked the window slightly more than it was. I reached into the glovebox and pulled out a bottle of Jameson.

CHAPTER 29.

Walking back in to the flat seemed strange. It had only been a week, but the place felt alien to me. Maybe it was knowing that Charlie wouldn't be coming back. She had only been in my life a short time and in her own unhinged way had changed everything. Not for the better to be fair but definitely different.

I started collecting the money together. Charlie hadn't known that I kept money in the flat. If she did it would of either gone up her nose or down her throat. I had hiding places all over. Just after I moved in, I had cut a hole in the plasterboard just left of the TV Ariel. I wrapped five thousand in a plastic bag and duct tapped it to the back of the wall. I then filled the hole and painted it. A well trained sniffer dog would probably have found it, but a burglar wouldn't. The rest had been tapped to the top of kitchen cupboards and various other places. I took the money back down to Nikoli and thanked him for his help and for the lift back from the airport and went back inside the flat.

After putting Exile on Main Street on the record player I finally slumped into the armchair with the bottle of Jameson, I had taken from Nikoli's car. Swigging from the bottle I worked out that I had a grand total of four thousand and twenty-six pounds left to my name and no job. The phone started to ring. I looked at the screen, it was a mobile number that I didn't recognise. I didn't normally answer them, but I needed to speak to someone. Even if they only wanted to tell me I had been in an accident. I lit a cigarette and pressed the green button.

'Ruben?' I hadn't even got out a hello.

'Charlie?' I was confused. I looked at the phone screen again. 'Where are you?'

'I'm still in Scotland. I wanted to make sure you were okay.'

'I'm fine. I've just got back from Rome. Is this your new number?'

'It's a borrowed phone so don't try to call back after. I wanted to check that Abdul had kept his side of the deal.'

'Yeah I've just sent the money to pay him off.' I said. 'Wait. What was the deal? What was your side?'

'That doesn't matter Ruben. None of this was your fault, you didn't deserve to be involved with those types of people.'

'Neither did you Charlie. I want to see you. I've been doing some thinking; I can move to Scotland or Kent or anywhere you want. I don't have a job here now and can work anywhere, it doesn't have to be London. Hopefully you'll choose Kent though, Scotland seems a bit cold and dark for me.'

'Ruben, think about it. We would never work now. You would always be second guessing where I was going or who with.'

'See that's where you're wrong. I'm not the jealous type.'

She sighed heavily. 'Problem is Ruben, I am. Despite all my lies you still cheated on me before you knew the truth. Before you knew what, I was.'

'That's not what you are Charlie, it's what you did to get by.'

'I love you Ruben, I really do, but this has to be goodbye.'

'But we could.' She cut me off. 'No, we couldn't. Move out of London like you said. Find a flat in Kent somewhere and enjoy life for a change. You are a good man.'

She was crying now. It was the first time I had heard her crying when she wasn't drunk.

'Goodbye Ruben. Thank you. I love you.' She hung up.

I smoked the cigarette down to the butt and lit another from the embers. I couldn't believe I wouldn't see her again. It obviously wouldn't work between us but just hearing her voice again made me miss her even more. I sat alone in my old leather chair and cried for the second time in as many days. It was disturbing the ease with which my tears came lately. I took a long swig from the bottle and stared blankly at the wall. Torn and Frayed was playing. I felt numb. I picked up the phone and pressed my Dad's number.

'Hello.' He answered just as I was about to hang up. It always took him an age to pick up.

'Dad, it's me.'

'Are you okay? Where are you?'

'I'm at the flat. I've handled that other business; you don't have to worry about it anymore.' I felt a sense of relief to say it out loud.

'Good. What do you want then? Sounds like you've been crying.'

'Do you know any flats or rooms for rent near you? Cheaper the better.'

'Why do you want to come out here? If it's all sorted up there you can stay in London surely.'

I heard my Mum say something in the background. 'What was that Mum said?'

'Your Mum told me to stop being an arse.' She was talking in his ear.

'Hello darling.' My Mum had taken the phone from him.

'How are you Mum?'

'Better than you from what your Father has told me. Should I still be expecting a visit from anybody?'

'I did ask him not to worry you with any of that. And yes, I've taken care of it.'

'You know him, two days of biting his nails to the base he had to tell me.'

'Mum, I want to move back down near you. Do you know of anyone who's renting a place out?'

'Actually, I do. A friend of mine at the Hospital, her son is a lovely boy. Well he is moving to Australia and is looking to rent his flat out. Doesn't want to sever all ties or something. It's down near the town centre. Nice place by all accounts.'

'Perfect. How much does he want?'

'Not a clue. I'll find out and let you know.'

'Thanks Mum.'

'Promise me no funny business. I don't want to face people at work if you've gone and done something awful to her son's flat.'

'I promise.' I said. 'Hand on heart.'

'As if that means anything you little shit. I'll call her now. And your Nan wants you to call her.' She hung up.

She was the only women who had never suffered any of my shit and who I could never lie to. She always told me straight, how I'd been an idiot. I loved her more than anyone else in the World and always regretted not making more of an effort to see or speak to her. I sat back in the chair and sipped the whiskey. It wouldn't be so bad living out in the suburbs again. I'd read in the Sunday paper sometime, ago about up and coming areas outside of London and Dartford's name was in the mix. I personally thought the place was a bit depressing. The town centre was grey and packed with single parents and young men with no shirts on acting like gangsters. The pubs and bars weren't much better. It's main claim to fame was the being the hometown of Keith Richard and Mick Jagger. They met on the platform of the train station supposedly. That and Henry V body was kept in the church after he shit himself to death in France before being taken on to London. I took the disc off the player and stood by the window and watched two Police officers questioning some kids. I'd miss London but I definitely needed the fresh start.

CHAPTER 30.

I had been living in the bright lights of the not so leafy Kent suburb of Dartford for around six months. Hand on heart, it wasn't as bad as I'd thought. I'd found a pub in the centre of town which was big enough to get lost in on a Sunday afternoon and also had a couple of seemingly genuine suppliers of narcotics. Although I had cut out the harder stuff altogether, they had a good selection of herbal remedies for the lonely evenings.

The flat that I was renting was on a nice quiet street. Nothing ever seemed to happen there. The first week I had moved in the Police had rung the entry phone. I panicked and flushed the cannabis before opening the door bleary eyed.

'Yes, Officer.' I said.

'Do you live here Sir?'

'I do. But not for very long. I moved in a little while ago. If it's a question about something before then I'd ring upstairs.' A nice gay couple lived upstairs. Brought me a cake down the first evening. We shared a couple of beers.

'Sir, are you okay?'

'Fine. I've just woke up. I'm on the night shift.' I wasn't working nights. I hate working nights.

'Apologies. Can I ask if you have noticed anyone hanging around the area in the last few days? Anyone out of the ordinary?'

I faked thinking for a few seconds. 'No Officer, I can't say I have. But like I said I'm on nights so, I'm normally asleep during the day.' Then Abdul's face appeared in my head. Or at least what I thought he may look like. 'Is there anything or anyone I should be concerned about?'

'Not really. We've had a few complaints of some mindless thug going around cutting the heads off people's flowers on the neighbouring estate. We're going door to door to see if anyone suspicious has been hanging around.'

I looked past him for the first time. There were three patrol cars and I counted five Officers.

'Business slow at the moment?'

'What do you mean?' He replied.

'Nothing. I really must go. Sorry I couldn't be of more help.'

I closed the communal door before he could answer and laughed to the point of barely being able to walk. The Kent Police force must have been bored to tears if it they had five Officers out looking for such a dangerous criminal mastermind. I could cope with living here if that was as bad as it got.

CHAPTER 31.

I had managed to pick up a job with a small refurb' company. They had a contract sprucing up the shops in the local precinct. These places never rented to one company for very long so were always being done up hoping for another poor bastard to pour their life saving into them. Sky high rent and only space for so many fast food shops normally killed many in the first half a year. That coupled with being on the doorstep of one of the largest shopping malls in Europe meant Dartford was a dying high street town. There wasn't even a Starbucks and those greedy fuckers will set up anywhere to hide some more tax money.

The work wasn't too strenuous. Removing old shelving racks and giving everything a coat of paint and a general clean up. As long as there were no accidents my contracts manager had no reason to visit. I'd spend most days reading and going to the pub for lunch.

I hadn't been near a woman since leaving London. After Charlie I just wanted to be alone. I was enjoying life and didn't need anyone, especially me, fucking it up. I had had the odd flirt at the bar. Maybe a cursory glance walking home but that was as far as I went. I'd go to work, then the pub for dinner and home in time to get my nine hours sleep. It was the life I had promised myself in Rome.

CHAPTER 32.

'Where's Dad?'

'He's over that bloody allotment.' My Mum hated the allotment. She always said she wished he'd have an affair like most other men. At least that would make him more interesting.

'Right, should have guessed.' I looked out of the conservatory window. The rain was bouncing off of the garden path.

'He'll be in that disgusting shed with that other moron Jim.'

'Never fancied joining him over there, Mum? Getting into the whole grow you own spirit?'

'No. The War finished a long time ago and rationing too. If I want vegetables or fruit, I'll go to bloody Sainsbury's like everyone else.'

'Does he not bring some of the stuff home that he grows?'

She was busy getting the Sunday roast ready. Roast potatoes are an art form that takes as many years to perfect as sculpting does. They need to have a light crisp on the outside while remaining fluffy on the inside. Many a roast have been fucked by a bad potato. Men and women the length and breadth of the country spend their Sundays in a near neurotic state because of this one thing.

She came back into the conservatory. 'Yes, of course he does. I give the dirty bloody stuff away to the neighbours and replace it with nice clean vegetables from the shops.'

'Fair enough.' I said sipping the coffee she had made me that was far too hot.

'So, tell me. How's the new job going?' She sat down next to me and smoothed the plastic table protector.

'Usual. There's not too much to say. I go in have lunch and leave.'

'Sounds interesting dear.' She had stopped listening.

I looked at her while she stared at the rain. She looked tired. I had a great admiration for her. Her work ethic made me look like a job shy arse. When I was young, she would spend the day-time being a Mum and looking after our home as well as cleaning other peoples houses that were too rich to do it their selves. Then when she had put me to bed and done my Dad's dinner after he had got home for work, she would put on a uniform and work in McDonalds for the evening shift. It was probably a shitty job for shitty money, but she did it anyway. I remember she would let me fall to sleep in her bed before she went out. My Dad would turf me out not long after. I pissed the bed as a child, so he obviously didn't want me in there for too long.

'Anybody of interest on the scene at the moment?' She asked without looking at me.

'Nope.' I replied. 'I told you I'm staying away from women for a while.'

'What about a man then? I didn't say a specific sex. It wouldn't bother me either way as long as you are happy.'

'Definitely no men in my life either Mum.'

'I'm just saying that after all the grief you've put yourself through with women maybe it's worth a change. My friend at work, her son is gay.'

'Doesn't really work like that Mum. I don't think you wake up one day and say, "well she was a bitch, so I think I'll have a bit of dick instead".' She smacked my arm and stood up laughing.

'What a way to speak to your Mother. Dirty boy.'

She went into the kitchen and returned a second later with a bottle of beer.

'Here, you look like that coffee has rat poison in it.'

'Thanks.'

'I just want you to be happy darling. And if swinging the other way would do it, I'll be more than happy to put in a good word with my friends son.'

'I'm fine, Mum. Thank you for caring so much though.'

She went back into the kitchen to check on dinner, happily whistling. I watched her through the conservatory doors. She was happy in the kitchen, alone, allowed to just get on with what she wanted. It was one of the times her and Dad clashed, when he tried to take over and say he had a better way of doing things. I heard the front door slam shut and my Dad appeared through the door to the kitchen. He kissed my Mum on the cheek and came into the conservatory.

'Fuck me, didn't take you long to help yourself to the beer.'

'Mum, got it for me actually.'

She passed him a beer over his shoulder.

'Did she ask you if you had turned Gay yet?' He said half laughing and taking a long hit from the bottle at the same time.

'Yeah, she mentioned it.'

'So, why are you here? I've already told you we haven't any money to lend.'

'I invited him for lunch, and he bought the joint of beef you'll quite happily finish off.' My mum cut in.

'Can I also say that I don't need your money, yet.'

'Is that the potatoes I can smell burning darling?'

My mum hurried into the kitchen. He smiled.

'How's work? Still down there in the town?'

'Yeah, it's going really well. There's talk of promotion.' That was a lie.

He nodded taking a sip of beer. 'That's great news. I told you moving down here would be a good idea.'

'I'm pretty sure your response was. "Don't come down here starting your old bollocks and asking for money." Unless you have a different recollection?'

He took a long swig from his bottle and stood up. 'Strange how the memory works. Another beer?'

'Please.'

CHAPTER 33.

'Listen, Ruben. I'm going to have to let you go.'

I should have known something was wrong when my boss had turned up unannounced. Ted was a nice man. One of the best managers I had had. He always rang ahead to give me the time to tidy up and make sure the men were behaving.

'Any particular reason?' I asked. He had lost his only son to cancer a few years ago and had never recovered. So was the rumour. Before he was a bear of a man. Grown men were terrified to be on the receiving end of one of his bollockings. Now he hated confrontation and people used that against him. It was sad.

'Some jobsworth in HR has an old colleague that works for your old company.' Never good. 'They mentioned that quite a bit of copper and materials went missing from a site you were running. There's nothing I can do, you're only on a temporary contract. I'm really sorry.'

I hadn't stolen the copper or materials but had taken a sixty percent cut of the money after I had found out who had taken it. It wasn't a shock that it had finally come back to bite me on the arse.

'That's fine, Ted. Don't feel bad.' I replied. 'How long do I have?'

'Straight away. The bosses aren't comfortable leaving you here without supervision. I'll have to cover for the time being until they can get me someone else.'

'What about pay?'

'You'll be paid till the end of the month. Again, I am sorry

Ruben. When you weren't in the pub you were a good manager.'

'Thanks Ted. For everything.' I stood up and shook his hand. I genuinely liked him.

'No worries. You have my email address so use me as a reference. I'll make sure it's a good one.'

I shook his hand again and looked around my desk for my personal possessions. There wasn't any so I made a big deal about putting a biro into my pocket.

Ted laughed. 'Got everything?'

I walked past and patted him on the shoulder. 'Thanks mate.' I said before leaving.

CHAPTER 34.

'Hi Charlie. I lost my job today. I know what you are going to say, but it wasn't entirely my fault this time.' I paused. 'Well technically it was. Looks like what you said was true, my past will catch up with me at some point. Anyway, hopefully we'll catch up soon.' I hung up.

I had been calling the number she had last called me from since the last time we had spoken leaving messages and just talking. It was one of the things that I missed about her. When the days became too black, I would lay on the bed with my head in her lap and pour my thoughts out while she stroked my hair. She never offered advice or criticism. She always said that wasn't her place. She just listened, which was enough. Now there was no one to listen so I rang her voicemail. I had no idea if she ever listened to the messages or even still used the number. In a way I hoped she didn't. I hoped she was happy even if I wasn't a part of that happiness.

I lit a cigarette and rested my head back on a pillow. Laying on the floor I stared at the cracks in the ceiling and blew a long stream of smoke towards the pendant light and tried to calculate how long I could last without a job. If I went easy I could possible string it out for a few months before I'd have to start selling my body parts.

I looked around the lounge, nothing was mine except the record player and creaking leather armchair I'd brought from the flat in North London. It was sad that I was almost in my mid-twenties and these few items were all I really owned. I turned my head and sucked the whiskey through a straw, it saved me having to sit up every time. My life hadn't exactly worked out how my parents had probably envisioned when I was a baby. I had never really had a master plan though other than making it to adult hood which I had achieved.

I lit a cigarette from the one I had been dangling from my lips. I took a long drag and held on to the smoke in my lungs. "Going to California" was playing. I thought of going to Los Angeles. I could try to get in touch with Lauren and ask her where's best to stay and things to do. I sucked at the whiskey. I'd sleep on it.

CHAPTER 35.

I hated interviews. I'd spend the night before in a panic and wouldn't be able to sleep. Then in the morning it would feel like I had an appendicitis. I would vomit at least twice.

The company were a Housing Association. The Government had sold or given, no one is quite sure which, most of what was left of the social housing stock they had left to these people to manage and generally fuck up on their behalf. A condition the Government had brought in was to force a brand new kitchen and bathroom on unsuspecting tenants. This is under the guise of the Decent Homes projects. A whole sub industry has built up around this where companies are making millions essentially carrying out DIY works and labelling them as proper construction.

I stopped being political a few years before. What this Government or the next spent our tax money on wasn't going to change because of a tick I put in a box. I used to vote. I had the same naïve belief that our Grandparents and great Grandparents were willing to die so we could have a freedom of choice in how we were governed. They didn't. Ask them. They were willing to die so the rest of the country wasn't slaughtered or turned into slaves by a group of self-loathing morons from the Reich.

In some ways I had always considered that a dictatorship would be easier. We would be saved the ritual of every four to five years being told that things are going to change, they won't. Vote for either side the outcome is the same. It takes so long to reverse what the last lot of arseholes have done; the new Government are voted out and we start all over again. The current Government is run by a University educated war-mongering millionaire and his not so attractive wife. Who can't decide which end to take it in from the Americans this week? And he is from the "Working class peoples party". Never done a hard day's work in his life. The prick on the other side is in some way related to the Royal Family. What chance do we honestly have? At least under a dictatorship you know life is going to be shit without having to get your hopes up. Another bonus to a dictatorship is that it cuts out the working class hero pop and rap stars giving us their insightful opinion on how the upper class are shitting on the lower class. All before stepping into their hundred thousand pound car and being chauffeured off to their Mansion in a Chelsea square with the closed off gardens. You stop being able to compare yourself with normal people when you have PA filling out your diary and booking flights to the Bahamas for you.

'Mr Humphrey. Mr Finnegan will see you now.'

'Thank you.' I said straightening my chinos. 'Where do I go?'

'Yes, sorry. Through the doors, first office on the left.'

I knocked on the door.

'Come.' It was all very 1960's.

I opened the door and stepped inside. Mr Finnegan was a big man, not in a fat way but definitely an ex-rugby player. Huge hands.

'Ruben, take a seat.'

'Thank you.' I said sitting down.

'What can you bring to Bailey and Motte that the next Manager cannot?'

The hard question straight from the off. A better company name I wanted to say. Instead I reeled off the usual answers.

'I'm a hard working person who isn't shy to get my hands dirty when I need to. I'm young enough to still have the desire to learn but old enough to have the maturity to run my own sites. I always lead from the front.' I was beginning to bore myself.

Everything that was spilling out of my brain was being jotted down in notes. Out of the blue he threw his pen on the desk and clasped his hands across his slightly obese stomach. Looking I could see sweaty skin through the gap between buttons. After nearly ten seconds of asking and answering his own questions in a barely audible noise he let a deep, almost sad sigh.

'I'll be straight Ruben. You're not the most qualified person I have seen today.' He turned his chair to face the window. I thought about slipping out. 'But I like you.' He finished before spinning back round slightly too fast and almost falling off the chair. He steadied himself and reached for a glass of water that was sat next to a pile of nut shells. I think cashew. Taking a sip and spilling most of it down the front of his ill fitted shirt. The buttons were now straining to hold together. I had only been in the room a few minutes, so fuck knows how he had come to the opinion that he liked me. I'd known myself for over twenty years and was still unsure about how I felt about me.

'I understand there are holes in my experience, but I will work as hard as anyone to fill them.'

He spilled some more water before placing his glass in the same place as before, turning it so the lines of the glass met perfectly with the lines of the desk. He sat and stared at me for a few seconds more.

'Let's do it.' He suddenly said.

'I have the job?'

'Don't let me down Ruben. I'm putting my bollocks on the chopping block here.'

He lent across the desk and offered his huge clammy hand. I shook it a bit too eagerly.

'It'll obviously be a three month probation period; I'll speak to HR and commercial to sort the starter packs and get you a company car issued. You can let go of my hand now.'

I hadn't realised I was still holding it. Now there was an uncomfortable atmosphere as I slid my hand from his.

'Thank you for this Mr Finnegan. I promise to work as hard as the next man and show you that I was the right choice.' I was making myself feel slightly nauseas.

He sat back in his chair. 'I'll be honest. You were the only person to apply that had actually been on a building site.' He bent down and pulled a small bottle of brandy from the bottom drawer and poured himself a large glass. He didn't offer me one.

'So, what was all that about me not being the most qualified person you had seen?'

'Listen I'm not trying to put you off, but we're grown men and we both know this isn't real construction.'

'You're not putting me off.' I couldn't give a fuck what we were or were not building as long as I was being paid.

'You'll be ripping out kitchens and bathrooms of some very ungrateful, disgusting shits. All they do is complain that something isn't good enough or that they are being put out by all the free work they're having done.'

He sank a little deeper into the chair. 'Trying to hire traditional site managers is near on impossible.' He downed the brandy and poured himself another. A little bit more than before. He had the demeanour of a man who wanted out. I scanned the photos around the room. Lots of handshakes with Mayors and councillors.

'So, how long have you been in Decent Homes Mr Finnegan?'

'Call me Steve and long enough.'

'It can't be all bad.'

He cut me off before I could finish. 'I used to work for a Tier 1 builder you know.'

'Why'd you leave? If you don't mind asking?'

'Lots of reasons. Stress, lack of desire to build characterless boxes for the rich to hide to their money. I had the idealistic view that I was giving something back by moving into this side of things. I was going to show that not all construction these days is about earning as much money as possible from putting in virtually fuck all.'

It was like being slapped across the ear. This overweight, sweaty man with nothing left to give was me in just a few wrong decisions. Within a decade I could be sat behind this shitty cheap desk wearing a shirt that was at least one if not two sizes too small and interviewing the only applicant for a job I loathed. I couldn't take it. If I did, I would probably end up on the roof cutting my wrists and jumping off.

He finally poured me a glass of Brandy and slid it across the desk.

'One thing I must say is try not to sleep with any of the residents.' He winked at me.

I sipped the Brandy and stared at him not knowing what kind of response he was looking for. I never really liked the taste of Brandy.

'We've had on occasions, Managers who have given extras for extras. If you know what I mean.' He winked again.

'I understand.' I said. 'But I'm not sure why you keep winking at me.'

'Let's just say it can be a sackable offense. It's a huge headache and a hell of a lot of paperwork for HR and legal.'

'Listen Steve.' I said downing the Brandy and sliding the glass back across to him. 'I can't guarantee that I won't do the same. Sorry.' I thought this could be my way out of having to take this shitty job without too much direct confrontation.

He let out a chuckle that only a fat man can. It was a mixture between Santa and a paedophile. Pouring out two more glasses of the cheap Brandy he passed me mine and winked again.

'We are only men. Who can resist the charming wiles of a young women when it's on a plate? I knew as soon as I saw you that you would fit in nicely.'

I'd done a lot worse, but this seemed disgusting and seedy. I didn't want to have any part of this. I'd have to go along with it until I got out of this office.

'Well where do I sign?' I said letting out a dreadful laugh and instantly wanted to take myself to the roof for a bit of wrist cutting.

'Good man Ruben. HR will have everything sent out to you tomorrow and I'll personally organise a rental car with a bit of room in the back.' He started laughing holding his stomach and winked at me again. I hoped he'd have a heart attack. 'I'll be in touch in a few days with a start date and site address.'

With that he chucked the Brandy down his huge wobbly throat and stood to attention.

'Thank you for coming in today Ruben.' I'd been in there less than fifteen minutes.

'No worries. Thank you for the opportunity.'

I left the office and made my way back to reception.

'How did it go?'

'I was offered the job.'

'That's fantastic news. Congratulations.' The receptionist was about my Mums age. I wondered if she knew what he was really like. Maybe he had tried to assert his authority on her. Maybe she didn't care as long as she was paid at the end of each month. 'So, we will be seeing a lot more of you around here then.'

'Highly unlikely. Your boss is a sexual deviant.' I pushed the entrance door open and stepped into the London sunshine. I had no idea what I was going to do next, but I couldn't work for that piece of shit. I put my Ray-bans on and lit a cigarette.

There were horror stories going around the construction industry of slowdowns and a recession coming. Companies weren't recruiting. We were always the first hit in any recession, Builders and Bankers. Bankers are always the ones blamed though. Slightly unjustified I think sometimes although ninety percent of them were pricks. I took out my phone and switched it back on. One voicemail message. I dialled 1 and listened.

'Ruben, I hope you're well. Although judging from the number of messages you've left me, I guess you could be better.' I crouched down against the wall. 'I wanted to let you know that I'm doing fine. In a way I'm glad you didn't answer. It makes it easier to hang up at the end. I'm sharing a little flat with my cousin. She found me a job waiting tables at the same restaurant as her, so I have money coming in.' There was a long pause. I thought she'd hung up. 'I miss you Ruben, I really do. Fuck, Milly told me not to call. I'm glad you didn't pick up. Remember the map we had? All the places we said we'd visit if we could get out of London. Promise me you'll do it on your own. Go and find yourself Ruben. God, I sound like all those horrible people you detest. You deserve to be happy. I'll always love you.' The message ended. I was crying almost uncontrollably. My nose was running. I sat against the wall and thought of calling her back. I missed her so much but knew she was in a better safer place. She would be happy in Scotland and I hated Scotland for that. I stood and wiped my eyes and nose. I took a long pull of the cigarette and flicked the butt into the kerb. Only children cry in the street my Dad would say.

CHAPTER 36.

I sat in a darkened corner of The Ship pouring over a map of Asia. The map Charlie had spoken about was long gone. I'd torn the flat apart looking for it. After a good few hours I'd given up and gone to a shop and bought another one. The first one had been from a copy of National Geographic. There had been an article about the spread of Buddhism from India into South East Asia. We had marked city's and countries that we thought would be good places to get drunk and high in. We had been very high at the time which is why I had forgotten all about the map until she mentioned it.

'Hey, I'm going to Asia.' I had said into the phone. The laughter that came back wasn't what I had been expecting.

'Why are you laughing for fucks sake? It's what I've wanted to do for a while.'

'I'll tell you what. I will pay for your flights if you go.'

'Why do you assume that I won't go?'

'Because you are like a scared little girl.'

'So, if I book it, you'll pay?'

'The thought of you in Asia is worth the money. You'll be shitting yourself into a coma within the week. And I mean literally shitting yourself'

'Fuck you then.'

'You wait till your Mother hears this one. Didn't you get dysentery on a trip to Dorset?' I hung up.

Taking a sip of my pint I traced my finger through India until I reached Goa. I'd heard stories of the hippy trail. I'd also heard stories of people basically being airlifted home because they had almost shit, their self to death. The thought of my dad laughing while I was wheeled through the airport and a nurse rubbing cream on my chapped arse sprang into my head.

'First trip?'

I looked up from the map. 'Yeah. I just don't know where to start.'

Daisy worked behind the bar. She was great with the drunks that rolled around on the floor most nights. She was early twenties, slightly grungy which was nice. I'd flirted a few times, but she never seemed interested. She had a very soft, kind voice. She grabbed the back of my hand and moved a few thousand miles to the right.

'Thailand?' I said.

'For your first trip I'm guessing outside of Europe I'd say yes definitely. It can be as intense or placid as you want it to be.' She picked up an empty from the table. 'India may kill you if you're used to sitting beside a nice clean pool and eating the buffet salad.'

'Ok. I have been to Tunisia though.'

'Mind how you go. All-Inclusive or half board?'

'All-Inclusive actually.'

'I don't mean to come across as condescending.'

'No, listen any advice is good.'

'Also depending on how long you plan to go for you can always cross into Laos, Cambodia or Malaysia. If you get really brave you could hike into Myanmar.'

'Where's that?'

'Where's what?'

'Myanmar? I've never heard of it.'

She looked at me. Trying to work out if I was being serious. I was. I'd never heard of it. I wasn't totally sure she was being truthful about a place called Laos.

'Burma. You've heard of Burma?'

'Yeah of course.'

'Well Myanmar is what Burma is called now.'

'Why?'

'The Military decided Burma was too Colonial or something.'

'Interesting. So not a fan of the British there then.' I put a line through Myanmar on the map. Abbie laughed and walked away carrying far too many glasses for her small perfectly shaped hands.

I went back to the map and concentrated on Thailand.

'Get yourself down to Waterstones and buy the book on South East Asia. It'll have everything you need to know.' Daisy had drifted back without me realising.

'What's the book called?'

She shook her head. 'The Book is called Lonely Planet. It has everything you need to travel safely and comfortably around different countries.'

'Sounds like a package holiday.'

'Just buy it and have a read. It has general prices and places to stay.' She sat down next to me. 'Is everything Ok at the moment Ruben?'

I focused on a place called Luang Prabang. 'Yeah why?'

'You seem very distracted lately.' She touched the back of my hand like Charlie would have. 'Did you get that job you were talking about?'

'Yeah, I got the job. I decided it wasn't the right fit for me.' I slid my hand from under hers.

'Why?' She asked.

'No reason. Can I get another beer and a whiskey on the side?'

'Sure darling. But no fighting tonight ok. I'm not cleaning your blood up again.'

I put an imaginary pin in Bangkok.

I didn't enjoy fighting; I wasn't very good at it. Unfortunately, it is the inconvenient side effect of spending too much time in a British Public House. On any given night of the week somewhere on our fair isles a poor fucker is having the shit beaten out of him, either inside or out. It didn't matter which to most. I avoided the loud, aggressive drinkers as much as possible. There is point however that all the avoidance in the World fails. A cursory glance in the wrong direction, a misplaced elbow and you finish your night in a pool of your own blood and vomit. If you are very unlucky there is always a night in A&E having glass removed from a part of your face and head. The wonderful British obsession of using a pint glass to end a disagreement.

CHAPTER 37.

'I listened to your message. I'm glad you're doing well, I really am. I took your advice and booked my ticket to Asia. I can't believe I'm going on my own. Not sure you remember but I'm not very good at small talk and worse at making friends.' I couldn't think of what to say. 'Thank you for contacting me. I cried in the street when I listened to the message. The dreams are back, and I can't remember the last time I slept properly. I miss you stroking my hair but that's me being selfish. Anyway, I leave on Tuesday at half nine at night. The girl who sold me the ticket said it'll be easier to get over the jetlag that way. I'm flying Thai Airways from Terminal 3 just in case you can make it.' I hung up.

I hoped that I would arrive at Heathrow just as she did, and we would run into each other's arms like they did in Hollywood and live happily ever after. Deep down I knew it was nonsense.

I knocked on my parents door and waited for my Dad to answer. He had asked me to come over before I left.

'So, you're really going?'

'I'm really going, yes. You paid the ticket.'

'I know I did, £800.'

'Thank you, Dad. I mean it.'

He passed me a bottle of beer and held it a little longer than necessary.

'I'm proud of you Ruben. I should say it more but that's not really me.'

'It doesn't matter.'

'It does to me, I love you son. You're my only child and I see you in pain and it kills me. I blame myself.' He took a long drink of his beer, which considering he'd started buying the little stubby bottle of French beers was quite a feat.

'Nothing I do is your fault Dad. It's just the way I am. I've come to accept it. I haven't killed anyone have I?'

'But you shouldn't have to accept it. We should have got you help when you were younger, but we didn't have the money for Therapists. And it was the 80's, they would have just locked you up.'

'Dad, seriously it's fine.' I didn't like to talk in this way. I finished the beer in two mouthfuls.

'How are the dreams?'

'Come and go. As always.'

'It's why you drink the way you do isn't it. It stops them. Gives you some peace.' He stood and walked back into the kitchen.

'What do you mean by that?'

'You won't remember but you told me once. You could barely open your eyes. You had been drunk for around three days straight.' He sat back down and passed me another bottle. 'You had stumbled through the door with piss stained trousers and one shoe. I laid on the bed and cuddled you like I would when you were a child and spent most nights screaming. I held you so tightly. You told me that drinking made them quiet. It made them leave you alone.'

I stood up and put my arms around his shoulders. He patted my elbow.

'Thank you.' I whispered.

'Please look after yourself out there and come back in one piece.'

'Of course, I will.' I kissed the top of his head and walked into the garden. He followed.

'What plant is that?' I pointed to a small pink flower.

'It's called Nerine. Comes from South Africa.'

I lit a cigarette and blew the smoke upwards, so it didn't drift back into the house.

'It's nice.'

'Make sure you give your Mum a kiss before you go. She'll be on my arse if you don't.' He gave my arm a squeeze and went back inside.

I flicked the butt over the neighbours fence and stepped back in the house to say goodbye. I didn't like goodbyes to my Mum. She would always make it into a last goodbye, even if I was going to the shops.

CHAPTER 38.

'So, you all packed?'

'Yeah I think so. Still have a few toiletries to buy and some sunscreen.'

'I wouldn't bother. It'll be cheaper once you get there.'

'What about proper Colgate? I can't brush my teeth with a local brand.'

Daisy laughed. 'They have Boots in Thailand you know. To be fair Boots is the best place to go when it's too hot.'

'I don't understand.'

'Has the best air-conditioning. You scared?'

'How can I be scared with my very own copy of The Book.' I waved a copy of South East Asia on a shoestring.

She smiled and walked to the other end of the bar to serve a regular. I didn't know his name. I had never bothered to learn. He was a pest. There was a little gang of them that would spend all day drinking through their own money before latching onto some poor fucker as they went to order at the bar. I'd told them to fuck off the first time they had tried it and given one of them a beating in the toilet. They left me alone after that.

'So, when's the flight?'

'Tomorrow.'

'Have you booked somewhere to stay when you arrive?'

'The Rembrandt.'

'Sounds posh. You didn't fancy The Khao San Road then?'

'I looked.'

'And?'

'And thought I'd treat myself for when I first get there.'

She laughed. 'It's your trip. Remember to do it how you want to. Not how someone tells you it should be done.'

'Exactly. I thought about staying somewhere a little more authentic. Then I took a look at some of the photos on the internet.'

'Like I say it's your trip. Just enjoy yourself. Whether you stay 1 month or 1 year.'

I left the pub a little while after. I hugged Daisy. I regretted it almost as soon as I had ceremoniously thrown my hands around her neck. She didn't show it, but I knew that it was as uncomfortable for her as me. I didn't know her that well and would probably have forgotten my name by the end of the week.

I had no idea what I was supposed to pack so, threw half a dozen t-shirts, some shorts and a couple of pairs of jeans in a rucksack. I sat on my chair and found my cigarettes and matches. I never used lighters when I smoked. I never had. I always preferred the taste and smell when you light a cigarette with a match. It takes you back to an older time when not everything had to be done at forty miles an hour. I rested my head back and for the first time that I could remember I felt quite peaceful. I chain smoked a few and drank a couple of large whiskeys. Bob Dylan was playing, I was relaxed.

CHAPTER 39.

Terminal 3 at Heathrow is a shithole. Heathrow may be one of the biggest, busiest airports in the World but none of the money fleeced from weary travellers was ever used for the upkeep of Terminal 3. From the minute you step inside the main checking hall you feel the sense of depression. Everything from the broken, stained ceiling tiles to the faded desks gave an impression of foreboding. That management didn't care if you lived or died as long as you didn't do it there. God knows how anyone could carry out a ten hour shift inside the dreary walls.

'Next.'

I stepped forward and handed my ticket and Passport to the very hopeful looking woman behind desk number four.

'Where are you travelling to today?'

'Does it not say on the ticket? Bangkok.' She looked at me with pure hate.

'Did you pack your bags yourself and has anyone ask you to carry anything through security on their behalf?'

'Yes and no.'

'Are you trying to be funny Sir? Airport security is not a laughing matter.'

'I'm not trying to be anything. I answered your questions. Did I packed the bag, yes. Has anyone asked me to carry something on their behalf, No.'

'Put your bag on the belt, please.' She almost spat the please part.

I did as I was asked without a word. She taped the sticker tabs around the handle and handed me back a boarding pass and my Passport.

'Have a nice trip. Next.'

I found a bar bought a couple of drinks and sought out a table near the back. I still didn't have the first idea of what I was going to do when I first arrived in Bangkok. Is there an itinerary to follow, certain places to visit. How many Temples can you visit in a day before they look the same. Surely there is only a given number of sights you can genuinely be interested in before you say, "Fuck it I can't take anymore" and disappear to the bottom of a bottle just for something to do.

I took out my guidebook and flicked through the photo's hoping for inspiration. I'd highlighted the Hotel on the map. Daisy had said to just get out there and see where the mood takes me. Making too many plans can ruin the experience and make it too packaged. Try to keep it as fluid as possible. Whatever that meant that's what I needed to do. From what I could gather being generally uncomfortable on a day to day basis was the main part of most people's enjoyment of travelling. I couldn't work out if that was an oxymoron or not. They felt connected to the "locals". Despite most of the "locals" would give their left leg to have a fraction of the monthly allowance a lot of the Backpackers had.

I looked around the bar at some of the other intrepid adventurers. Most looked happy, they weren't anxious about going to shores unknown. They revelled in the chance to discover the uncharted. To search out new experiences and try the untested. I was fucking terrified that the hotel wouldn't have hot water.

'Excuse me. Do you mind if I sit here? The bar's a bit busy.'

I turned my head. 'Of course not, please.' I made a hand gesture towards the seat opposite.

'So where are you off to today?' She asked.

A slightly forward question I thought. 'Thailand to start off with.'

'Snap. Ever been before?'

'Never.'

'Me neither. I'm a little nervous to be honest. My parents didn't want me travelling alone but I assured them I wouldn't talk to strangers.' She laughed while sipping her drink.

She was a stunning girl. I guessed 5 feet somewhere under half-way, brown hair to her shoulders and tanned skin. She could have been mixed race from years gone by. I looked down at her feet. She was wearing slightly faded blue Converse.

'I'm sure you'll be fine.' I took a sip of my beer. 'Have you booked anywhere for when you arrive?'

'No. I'm going to get a Taxi into the Koh San Road and check into a hostel. That's where all the others will be.' She seemed very pleased with herself. 'How about you?'

I didn't want to tell her. It may break her spirits and she was so sure that staying in a hostel was the proper way of backpacking. 'I checked out a few of those places but ended up booking a hotel on Soi Sukhumvit. So, you are meeting friends then?'

'No why?'

'You said "the others" will be at the Koh San Road.'

'Sorry I meant other backpackers. I wasn't being literal.' She scanned the bar for someone more interesting who could save her from the prick she had had the misfortune to have sat next to.

'It's not that I won't be staying in hostels. I just wanted a decent room to get over the jet lag.'

She half grinned still looking around. 'It's your holiday. You want to stay in five star hotels or back street brothels it's up to you.'

'Actually, it's only three stars. It doesn't even have a pool.'

She laughed. Too loudly. 'How will you live without a spa to wallow in?' I laughed as well.

'Can we start again?' I said.

'Why do we need to start again? Do you have some plans for us in the future?' She drank what was left in her glass.

'Can I buy you another?'

'Please. Gin and Tonic.'

I walked to the bar and ordered. I watched her from my covered viewing point. Not in a stalker way but to try and get an idea of the type of girl I was dealing with. I drank a quick short while I waited for the G&T. She talked to herself when alone. I liked that.

'Hi I'm Ruben. Do you mind if I sit down?'

She smiled at me. Her deep brown eyes holding mine. I couldn't look away.

'I suppose you could sit down till my companion comes back. You never know he could be a while.'

I sat opposite her still keeping eye contact. I'd never liked eye contact. I haven't got Asperger's or anything, I just found it uncomfortable. A voice in my head told me if I looked away, she would disappear.

'I'm Charlotte.' She said

'Ruben.'

'I know. You said that already.' She sipped the G&T through the straw She had beautiful teeth. 'So, what happened?'

'What do you mean?'

'Well you left the table a bit of a wanker. If you don't mind me saying. Now you seem different.'

I wanted to say that I felt like I was in love with her. She reminded me of Charlie and Lauren. Of every woman I'd ever met. She made me feel at ease.

'I feel like I know you already. Where are you from?'

'Kent. You?'

'Yeah near there. Where abouts?'

'A place called Bobbing. You wouldn't have heard of it. No one ever has.'

I hadn't so, didn't bother trying to make something up. I sank my drink in a panic.

'Can I buy you another?' I asked.

'I reckon I'll be Ok.' She tapped the side of her still full glass. 'I'm not a huge drinker. You should have a soft drink. It's a long flight.'

I went back to the bar and ordered a double whiskey.

Printed in Great Britain
by Amazon